"Be careful.
Big-corporation heads are
susceptible to
those wide golden eyes of yours
and to your seductive body."

"Take your hands off me!" Rea cried.

Moving deliberately, he pulled her against him and brought his mouth down on hers. The touch of his lips on hers filled her with a desire that left her giddy and defenseless against his mouth and lips and bold, probing tongue. She could taste him, smell the scent of his after-shave, feel the strength of his tall, powerful body pressed against hers.

Then he stepped away from her. "It's really too bad. Your . . . er . . . technique is excellent. I am sure you'll get all the interviews you want."

Dear Reader:

We've had thousands of wonderful surprises at SECOND CHANCE AT LOVE since we launched the line in June 1981.

We knew we were going to have to work hard to bring you the six best romances we could each month. We knew we were working with a talented, caring group of authors. But we *didn't* know we were going to receive such a warm and generous response from readers. So the thousands of wonderful surprises are in the form of letters from readers like you who've been kind with your praise, constructive and helpful with your suggestions. We read each letter... and take it seriously.

It's been a thrill to "meet" our readers, to discover that the people who read SECOND CHANCE AT LOVE novels and write to us about them are so remarkable. Our romances can only get better and better as we learn more and more about you, the reader, and what you like to read.

So, I hope you will continue to enjoy SECOND CHANCE AT LOVE and, if you haven't written to us before, please feel free to do so. If you have written, keep in touch.

With every good wish,

Sincerely,

Carolyn Nichols

Carolyn Nichols
SECOND CHANCE AT LOVE
The Berkley/Jove Publishing Group
200 Madison Avenue
New York, New York 10016

P.S. Because your opinions *are* so important to us, I urge you to fill out and return the questionnaire in the back of this book.

GARDEN OF SILVERY DELIGHTS

SHARON FRANCIS

A
SECOND CHANCE AT LOVE
BOOK

GARDEN OF SILVERY DELIGHTS

Distributed by Berkley/Jove

First edition published April 1982

First printing

Printed in the United States of America

Second Chance at Love books are published by
The Berkley/Jove Publishing Group,
200 Madison Avenue, New York, NY 10016

- 1 -

"TIRED? HOW COULD I be tired? Tucker, I'm just realizing that I'm finally in Japan!"

Though faint smudges of weariness under Rea Harley's hazel eyes contradicted her words, her voice was vibrant with interest. The middle-aged man beside her shook his head anxiously.

"You're sure my dragging you to the Royal Hotel isn't too much for you? It's a long way from Boston to Osaka! I wish there'd been some way of dropping you off at home before coming to this sword ceremony, but my best staff writers all have assignments, and I needed to cover the story for *Outlook*."

Rea's eyes turned almost golden when she smiled, and the glint of hotel chandeliers caught her honey-brown hair so that her heart-shaped face also seemed framed in gold. "Tucker, quit worrying about me. I couldn't have asked for a better welcome. A ceremony involving a samurai sword . . . and a Japanese baron, too!"

She gazed around her at the enormous lobby of the Royal Hotel. A huge picture window near them framed a magnificent waterfall. Rivulets from it cascaded over the rocks of the fall, then streamed in a river that flowed through the lobby. With her eyes on the sun-dazzled water, Rea spoke softly.

"It's as if a dream I've been dreaming for a long time has come true. You and Janet know that, Tucker. Before I married Bill, I used to talk about nothing but coming to Japan—"

Tucker interrupted her. "Rea, about Bill. Jan and I figure you were too good for him. Always were. I only wish you'd come to us last year, right after the divorce. I know it's been rough for you."

"That's all over now." Rea turned and pretended to study the stream of water at her feet. She wished she'd never brought up Bill's name. Tucker and Janet Wynn had always been like an aunt and uncle to her, even more so since her parents' death some years back. Tucker's concern was genuine... but that didn't make talking about Bill any easier. "How's Jan's practice?" she continued lightly. "I'll bet she still works too hard."

"You know her, the old family doctor! Now that she has a clinic of her own, she's hardly ever home, always running around after her patients." Tucker patted his comfortable waistline. "Me, I could use some running around. Journalism is a good life, Rea. You should've gone into writing instead of teaching."

"I'm glad *you* went into writing. I'm going to ask you for help with my book, Tucker... as editor of *Far East Outlook.*"

"Me advise an assistant professor of social history? Wait a sec, though. Maybe I *can* help. I'll introduce you to Jun Akira after the ceremony."

"The baron?"

"His son. The old Bamboo Baron is in Paris on business, so his only son will be standing in for him at the ceremony today. The story of the sword itself might interest you, Rea. It seems that a very old and valued samurai sword was stolen from the House of Akira during World War Two. The family spent a lot of time and money tracking it down, and finally succeeded. The American Ambassador is returning it today, after several remarks about friendship between our two countries." He paused. "At least, that's the official story. Actually, the sword was found months ago, but the baron was waiting for a good time to have the ceremony."

"And this is a good time?" Rea asked. The last of her weariness fell away as Tucker spoke. Some hotel employees were clearing a space before the picture window, arranging a small portable dias and several large baskets of flowers. The mingled scents of roses, carnations and pine filled the air.

"Sure it is. He's publicity-hungry right now, see. He's

trying for a big new market in the U.S. of A., for some of his electronic components. All this 'friendship between two countries' stuff will get him plenty of press coverage here and abroad."

Rea pulled a camera from her large shoulder-bag. "I'm going to photograph the ceremony. Maybe I can use it as a preface to my book. But . . . could Baron Akira's son really help me with my writing?"

"And how. He could introduce you to big wheels in industry." Tucker winked. "That is, if he takes a liking to you."

"Oh." In her mind, Rea conjured up a fussy, middle-aged aristocrat turned businessman. She'd never met a real baron before, let alone a Japanese one. How to please a person like that? She half turned to ask Tucker, when a mild commotion caused her to turn towards the hotel entrance. Tucker nodded as waiting journalists and camera people hurried into position and waiting guests craned their necks to get a better view.

"Here they come," Tucker said.

Two hotel employees flung wide the Royal's doors. A gray-haired man in formal attire walked in first. The Ambassador, Rea thought, lifting her camera for a shot. Then she lowered the camera, her eyes wide with surprise. Beside the Ambassador strode the most extraordinary-looking man she'd ever seen.

He was easily six feet tall and was dressed in ancient Japanese court costume: short, dark ceremonial kimono and *hakama,* long, loose silk trousers which flowed from a narrow waist to a sweeping width at the base. In such a costume anyone might attract glances, but this man would have been a standout anyplace he chose to go! Though his hair was the smooth black hair of a Japanese, and his skin a warm olive, his features were European. So were the emerald-green eyes that swept the throng of press and guests with an easy interest. For an instant, those extraordinary eyes met hers, and dark, bold eyebrows rose. Then his lips quirked up at her and he nodded his proud head at her slightly before sweeping past them all into the reception area beyond. Rea caught her breath—this man was amazing.

"Jun Ivan Akira," Tucker whispered. He was grinning at Rea's reaction. "The son of the Bamboo Baron and a Russian singer. Tell you more later," he added.

The Ambassador had stepped up on the dias, and a hush fell over the crowd. He described the soldiers who'd taken the sword, and the efforts of the Akiras to locate it. Then an aide handed him a long, graceful ceremonial sword. Rea yearned to hold it in her hands. How much history had that sword seen? She watched eagerly as the Ambassador presented it to Jun Ivan Akira, who, after a low formal bow, began to speak.

Another surprise. Rea had thought he would speak in Japanese and had been readying her knowledge of the language. She was astonished when the baron's son began his speech in perfect English. "In our country, we often rely on symbols to convey our feelings," he said. "The Akira family begs the Ambassador of the United States to accept our small gift of rare Japanese chrysanthemums, which will be sent to the American people. It is our hope that the flowers will symbolize peace, goodwill, harmony and good fellowship between us . . ."

". . . As well as profit margins," Tucker whispered in Rea's ear.

Rea hardly heard him. She watched, fascinated, as the baron's son slid the samurai sword into place at his side.

"Looks like somebody out of *Shogun,* doesn't he?" A breathy voice murmured beside Rea. Looking around quickly, she saw a blonde woman with heavily made-up eyes. "Tucker, you bad boy," the woman continued before Rea could answer. "You've been hiding out on us. *When* did you get a new secretary? *Much* better than that sour old battleaxe, Mrs. Enno. What does Janet have to say?"

Tucker grinned. "Babette Lane, from the English *Daily,"* he explained to Rea. "Don't get excited, Babette. Rea's an honorary niece of Jan's and mine. She's an assistant professor at Reece University in Boston. Here to write a book about social history. Japan in transition, you know."

"How fascinating." The sharp eyes looked disappointed, and Rea was amused. "You must tell me what a social historian does."

"Well, we study how people are affected by social interaction," Rea began. Seeing boredom descend on the reporter's features she added wickedly, "I'd really love to tell you all about it, Ms. Lane. The book I'm writing will deal with the cultural patterns in Japan, the rapid growth of industry and its affect on old traditions, the family . . ."

"Fascinating!" Babette grabbed Tucker's arm. "Come on, Tuck. Let's get some champagne and hors d'oeuvres before that rat pack devours every drop and crumb!" She steered him quickly away from Rea, who couldn't help but chuckle as Tucker winked broadly at her.

"Do you really mean to do all that, or were you just trying to impress the formidable Miss Lane?"

Surprised by the rich voice, Rea found herself looking up into the clearest green eyes she had ever seen. Sea green, she thought, the kind of color you sometimes find in beach glass. The baron's son was smiling down at her, but there was a hint of mockery in the tilt of his dark brows.

"I really did mean it," she said. When he merely kept on watching her, she heard herself adding, "I know I've got to work hard at it, since I have very little time. Luckily, I work best under pressure."

"You are new here. I haven't seen you before, otherwise I would have remembered you." She introduced herself, and the eyebrows rose fractionally. "You are a friend of Tucker Wynn?"

Rea realized with annoyance that she was being mistaken for Tucker's girlfriend again. "Jan and Tucker were friends of my parents," she said, and wondered why she felt tense, somewhat off balance. To mask her insecurity, she deliberately assumed her cool, clipped, professorial voice. "Mr. Akira, Tucker mentioned that you and your family are extremely well known in industrial circles. I wonder if it would be possible to visit your firm, perhaps interview you . . ." Her words trailed off as he laughed. She frowned. "Did I say something funny?"

"You must excuse me." There was more than a tinge of mockery in his voice this time. "You see, we get all kinds of writers here in Japan. Most of them wander around harmlessly enough. They attend tea ceremonies and sit in bars or move around the countryside, soaking in culture. Most of them don't bother with such dry subjects as industry, especially if they are young and lovely."

Rea felt her cheeks grow warm, and cursed the fact that she was probably the last woman on earth to blush easily. A waiter came up to them, bowing and offering a tray of champagne, and Ivan Akira selected two glasses. "You look warm," he murmured, offering Rea a glass. Their fingers touched as she took the glass, and the casual warmth of his touch made her cheeks feel still hotter.

"I really intend to write my book, Mr. Akira," she said, as evenly as she could. "I'm serious about requesting some of your time. I know it's an imposition, but . . . if you like, I could send you a letter with my credentials." Again he said nothing, but just sipped his champagne, as he watched her with that clear green gaze of his. "Japan isn't a . . . a passing interest for me, you see. I was interested in the country when I was in grade school, and an exchange student from Japan lived with my family while I was in high school. I majored in Far Eastern history in college, learning the language . . ." He still didn't reply, so she added, "Of course, if you'd rather, I won't pursue the matter."

He lifted his champagne glass, toasting her lightly. "I'm sure you'll be an enormous success. professor." He was stopped from saying more by Tucker, who returned at this moment with a napkin full of hors d'oeuvres.

"So you two have met," he said cheerily. "That was a fine speech, Mr. Akira. I'm going to quote you in *Outlook,* all right?"

"By all means." The baron's son was all politeness. "You'll excuse me? I have to go and talk to the Ambassador." He paused. "There will be a dinner at the Kin-Bara restaurant tonight, by the way. I wonder if you and Dr. Wynn can come? And by all means, bring the lovely professor with you."

He strolled off without waiting for an answer, and Rea found herself staring after him. She didn't know whether to laugh or be irritated. "Well!" she finally exclaimed, then laughed and shook her head. "A command performance, no less!"

"That's the Akira style. What do you want from the man?

He's the richest eligible bachelor in these parts. He acts as if he doesn't take anything or anyone seriously, but don't you believe it. Behind those handsome green eyes is a deadly-serious brain."

"Really." Rea couldn't help following Ivan with her eyes, and as if in recognition of the fact, he turned and smiled at her. There was a curious warmth in the smile, a hint of intimacy, in spite of its accompanying touch of mockery. Rea recalled the touch of Ivan's fingertips, then brushed away the memory. "Are you going to that dinner of his?" she asked Tucker.

"If you're not too tired, it'd be an experience. It'd be your initiation into Japanese social life . . . *and* a respectable geisha party!" He glanced at his watch. "We'd better get out of here, Rea. If I don't have you home soon, Janet will never forgive me."

Rea followed Tucker out of the Royal Hotel. Outside, without the benefit of air conditioning, the June heat reminded her of her fatigue. After all, she'd spent more than fifteen hours in the air! She was grateful to climb into Tucker's Renault and lean back against the car seat. She closed her eyes, but Tucker was in a talkative mood.

"If I were you, Rea, I'd write a chapter about people like the Akiras. I don't mean just in a business sense, either. There's a blend of culture in Ivan Akira . . . East and West. I told you that his mother was a Russian singer. Alexandra Ivanovna—ever hear of her?"

Rea shook her head. Her eyes kept trying to close, but she wanted to hear Tucker's story and also take in everything about her. Perhaps because she was so weary, it seemed as if her senses were acutely aware of everything about her—the heat, the smell of exhaust and leather, the green, fan-shaped leaves of the gingko trees which lined the highway.

"Alexandra was an opera singer. Not in a class with Galli-Curci and the like, but very good. She came to Japan on tour, and the Bamboo Baron fell in love with her. He even went through a morganatic marriage with her. It wasn't official, of course. His family would have died of shame if their only son had married a non-Japanese."

"You mean those old ideas have survived into this century?" Rea asked. "Japanese can still only marry Japanese?"

"Well, things are somewhat easier now, but many families today—especially proud, wealthy families—wouldn't stand for intermarriage! Even so, the baron couldn't resist Alexandra. She was tall, golden-haired and beautiful. The Japanese called her 'Kin Bara,' the Golden Rose."

Tucker slowed for a signal, and Rea felt her eyelids fold down over her weary eyes. From far away, Tucker was still speaking. "Eventually, the baron had to take a legal wife to please his family. He married a wealthy noble woman, and they had a daughter, Midori. The baron still adored Alexandra, though, and he was devoted to her and their small son. When the legal wife died, there was talk about the baron's marrying his Golden Rose. There was a big brouhaha about it, and Alexandra solved the problem by going back to Russia. She died there." He paused. "Ivan must have been about ten when his mother left Japan."

"You mean she left him here and went away? Poor little boy!"

Tucker snorted. "I wouldn't call him poor, Rea! He's had the best education . . . Oxford, then Harvard Business School for his M.B.A. The baron adopted him legally, groomed him for the business, and so he's also had power, money, prestige and position! You name it, that man has got it!"

Rea drowsily thought of Ivan Akira, and how his green eyes had met hers. The memory caused a thrill to run through her, and she smiled. He certainly has got it all, she thought. He most certainly has!

- 2 -

REA DROPPED OFF to sleep on Tucker's last words. When she did open her eyes again, they were in the suburbs outside Osaka City, turning onto a narrower road that led to the Wynns' apartment. Rea was a little disappointed that the building was the typical high-rise so common now in Japan, about as traditionally Japanese as one of the "MacDonald" stands she saw as they turned the corner.

She sighed. She had known, of course, that land was at a premium in Japan and that many of the "old" Japanese homes had been replaced by apartment complexes and parking lots. But she would have given anything to have the Wynns live in a small, tatami-matted Japanese dwelling. Her disappointment didn't last long, however. When they got out of the car, Rea saw Janet Wynn standing on a balcony high above her, waving both arms.

"Thank heavens Tucker finally brought you home!" Janet shouted. "Good Lord, a *sword* ceremony, and the girl half dead with jet lag? Come in right this minute, before you say another word!"

"You haven't changed," Rea laughed with a catch in her throat as she and Janet embraced a few minutes later. "It's so good to be here, Jan!"

"Let me look at you!" Janet ordered with tears in her eyes. "You haven't changed either, child."

Oh, but she had, Rea thought, and felt a wave of weary sorrow roil through her. Tucker interrupted as he carried her suitcase out of the elevator.

"My God, Rea, what have you got in this thing? Bricks?"

"Just my tape recorder and books. . . . I'm sorry it's so heavy, Tucker. You *did* say I could rent an electric typewriter here?" she added anxiously as Tucker preceeded them into the apartment.

"Already done, my dear!" Janet gestured. "How do you like the Wynn hotel?"

Rea stood in the doorway, charmed. The small apartment was a mixture of East and West. The floor was wooden, but a grass mat had been spread over it, and though the furniture was Swedish modern, the ornaments and pictures on the wall were Oriental. One magnificent scroll dominated a white wall, and Rea quickly walked over to study it. It was deceptively simple, with bold black calligraphy forming a bridge of Japanese characters on the white paper.

"It's a Nando," Janet explained. "A wealthy patient gave it to me. Now, Rea . . . you have got to eat something and then go to bed and sleep for hours and hours. Doctor's orders."

Tucker explained about the party at the Kin-Bara restaurant. Janet looked doubtful. "What do you think, Rea? You might feel all right now, but jet lag will hit you soon. My daily help, Kazuko, left some cold chicken and salad for our supper. Wouldn't that be better . . . chicken and talk and sleep?"

Rea hesitated. Janet was right, and yet *talk* was the last thing she wanted now . . . at least, talk about Bill! And there had been the challenge of Ivan Akira's bold green eyes. "I wouldn't want to miss my first geisha party," she said. "I'm fine, Jan, really. All I need is a cold shower and a short rest. I used to be on the run a lot, you know, when . . . when I was with Bill."

Bill's name dropped into the conversation and lay there heavily. Janet looked at Rea closely, then gave her another quick hug. "Okay, why not?" she said. "But I insist you lie down before we go. We can talk anytime, after all. You'll be here for months!"

She ushered Rea into a small, comfortable guest bedroom, then led the way to the bathroom. Gratefully, Rea stripped off the navy-blue silk blouse and white slacks she had worn while traveling, and stepped into the shower. As the blissfully cold needles of water hit her hot skin, she closed her eyes and forced her mind to clear itself of memories. She was in Japan, and she was going to write a book.

It was a new venture, one she had wanted to undertake all her life. It was a new beginning.

She lathered soap in her hands and began to wash her slender, high-breasted body, letting the cold water cascade down her gently rounded hips and long, slim legs. "I'm really here," she whispered aloud. "Today I watched a sword ceremony. Tonight I'll go to a grand dinner. And Ivan Akira will be there. . . ."

She stopped talking, annoyed at herself for thinking about Ivan Akira as though he were the reason for her going tonight! But how vivid the man had been. It was extraordinary, but she could visualize him near her, feel the tips of his fingers brush hers. She remembered how those sea-green eyes had watched her, and was suddenly and acutely aware of her creamy naked body and the hardening of her nipples. Hurriedly, she finished washing her hair, and began to towel herself dry.

"There's only one reason I want to meet that man again tonight," she told herself. "I'm going to ask him about that interview again." That was businesslike enough, certainly! Her next thought was not. "What am I going to wear?" Rea asked herself aloud.

She had traveled light, a habit acquired during her marriage to Bill Delahey, a freelance photographer whose job often forced them both to pack and move at a moment's notice. In her suitcase were books, jeans and T-shirts, a few cotton dresses and her "good" business suit for interviews, Then she remembered the impulse that had caused her to toss her one cocktail dress on top of the heap. It was all she had, and would have to to do, even though it was nothing fancy or elegant. Perhaps that was all to the good. Perhaps Ivan Akira would take her more seriously if he realized she wasn't a giddy social butterfly.

Rea had never been one to dawdle over "dressing up." After a short rest, she quickly blow-dried her hair and put on the cocktail dress. It was very simple . . . too simple, she thought as she critically surveyed herself in the dresser mirror. She wished she had brought along jewelry, something to lend romance to the close-fitting dress with the side slit and the rounded neckline. Then she caught herself up sharply. Romance be hanged! What was needed tonight was her portable tape recorder, her camera and her notebook. That was what was most important.

And yet . . . "I *have* changed," Rea murmured, staring at her face in the mirror. There were the shadows under her hazel eyes, the faintest of worry lines between her eyebrows. Her mouth, too, had altered. Once it had been soft, rounded, ready to whisper love words and be kissed. Now her lips were firm, unsmiling. Rea tried a smile, and saw that it only gave her face a tremulous vulnerability.

Three months was all she had. No, not even that . . . just seventy-two days. And in that time, she needed to write her book. It was publish or perish, in the words of the very true old cliché. For just a second she allowed herself to visualize a future without the tenuous, newly-won security of her job.

"I will write my book," she said out loud. "I'll make sure Ivan Akira helps me, too."

"Talking to yourself, hey?" Janet stuck her head in the doorway. "Almost ready?" She watched as Rea packed camera, recorder and notebook into a shoulder bag. "You look like a mighty pretty camera lady."

Rea looked up and caught the look of understanding in Janet's eyes. It'll be all right, the look said. Her moment of fear receded, and she felt a warm rush of confidence. "I'm ready for anything," she said with a laugh. "Bring on the geisha girls!"

By the time they reached the outer gates of the Kin-Bara restaurant, she was happy and excited. The first sight of the restaurant itself made her clap her hands. "It's like a Japanese house!" she exclaimed.

"You used to see this sort of building all over Japan," Janet said as Tucker drove the car through the outer gates and up a winding gravel road shaded by stately Japanese pines. "You know who owns this place? The Akiras. The old baron named it after Alexandra. The Golden Rose."

The car slid to a halt in front of a typical Japanese *genkan*, or entryway. A young man in white shirt and dark trousers bowed deeply, intimating he would park the car. *"Irashiai-mase,"* he said, bowing even lower. "Welcome."

Rea followed the Wynns through the genkan, listening to the soft voices and laughter that could now be heard. A flagstoned outer entryway led to a stone step. Paper-and-wood screens slid open above the step, and three young Japanese women in butterfly kimono knelt on the woven tatami matting, bowing. *"Irashiai-mase,"* they chorused as they helped the guests off with their shoes, then offered them slippers. They led the Wynns and Rea down a wooden corridor to an inner room and yet another paper-and-wood screen door.

"Dozo," one of the girls said, softly. "Please." She went down on her knees to slide open the screen, and bowed to the floor as Rea and the Wynns stepped past her and into the room beyond.

Rea's first impression was that every inch of the large room had been skilfully used. The result was that even though there were many people in the room, it did not seem crowded. The guests were seated on cushions around a long, low rectangular table. Rea instantly picked out Ivan Akira. He was wearing a dinner jacket and was bending over to speak to a young, petite Japanese woman in a yellow kimono. She also recognized the Ambassador, with a woman who must have been his wife. They were seated in front of the *tokonoma,* the place of honor, marked by a scroll painting and an arrangement of flowers. The Akira sword had been reverently placed beneath the scroll.

Babette Lane was there, too. She waved at the Wynns and Rea as they took their seats. Rea returned the wave, then found herself glancing again at Ivan, who was now listening to the Ambassador's wife. His face was in bold profile, but before she could look away, he had turned, his clear green gaze seeking hers for a second before he returned his attention to the other woman. Rea felt her cheeks burn at the interest she had read in that split-second look.

There was now a stir in the room. The maids had ushered in two remarkable-looking women. Dressed in elaborate kimono, their faces painted, and coiffed in the ancient way, the geisha walked slowly and delicately towards the place of honor to make their obeisance to the Ambassador. One geisha carried a drum, the other a long, banjolike instrument.

"A *shamisen!* And honest-to-God *shamisen!*" Rea breathed. "I remember researching shamisen for a paper I wrote long ago."

Then the feast began. The maids poured hot Japanese *saké* into Rea's thimble-small cup, slid dishes of food in front of her. Watching the geisha attend the guests of honor, Rea sipped her hot *saké* and tasted salads of radish, sliced cucumber and ginger root, hors d'oeuvres of abalone, caviar, skewered beef and chicken and pork, grilled fish the size of her forefinger, white lotus root and tender chunks of bamboo shoot.

Dish after dish was placed before Rea. A magnificent seabream, its eye glaring defiantly, was placed whole and dripping with pungent sauce in front of her. Kobe beef followed, so tender that it could be cut with chopsticks. Other dishes came and went, and between the food and the wine, Rea was satiated. Feeling marvelously relaxed and light-headed she took several photographs of the geisha and guests, including a shot of the *tokonoma* with the sword and the flowers.

She was changing her film, when a deep voice behind her asked, "Are you having a good time, professor?"

Ivan knelt on one knee behind her, and she reflected that he looked as imposing in Western dress as he had in ancient Japanese clothes.

"I'm having a lovely time," she said.

"Let's hope everything in Japan is as pleasant," he said, courteously, though his eyes danced with subtle mockery. "I see you have been busy taking pictures. Are you talented in photography as well as social history?"

"I used to work with photographs when . . . a long time ago," she said. "I intend to use many photographs in my book."

"Ah, your book! I am impressed." He didn't look it, however, Rea thought, and again felt the surge of irritation mixed with fascination that she had experienced earlier. The wine she'd drunk made her bolder than usual. Now or never, Rea. Go for it!

"Are you impressed enough to let me come and talk to you at Akira Industries? It would mean a lot of good publicity for you," she added, recalling what Tucker had said about the baron. "I'll be sure to give Akira Industries credit in my book."

"That would be too much of an honor." He didn't say

yes or no, and Rea felt she couldn't press him further.

"I'll send you some of tonight's photographs," she was beginning, when one geisha began to clap her hands and call out, *"Tanko-bushi!"*

There were groans from the guests, also comments, clapping and laughter. Several of them stood up and began to form a line behind the geisha. Rea looked at Ivan for explanations.

"You mean you don't know? Shame on you, Professor Rea." Her pulse leaped as he spoke her name, softening it, the sound of his voice a caress she could almost feel. His green eyes were intent upon her, and she had to force herself to concentrate on what he was saying. "It's a folk dance, the tanko-bushi. It takes place in a coal-mining town. The miners toil under a full moon, and they sing as they work."

Tucker and Janet had joined the now-moving line. The dancers stepped forward clapping hands, back-stepped and then went on again. Rea could see that the gestures they made implied the digging of coal and the pushing of coal carts.

"It doesn't look so hard," she ventured.

"Then come . . . try it!" Before she realized what he was doing, he had reached out and grasped both her hands, pulling her to her feet. For a second, his warm, strong hands held hers, and again she was conscious of the intensity of his remarkable eyes. Then he had maneuvered her into line and placed himself behind her.

Rea's head whirled with saké, the music, the dance. She began to move with the others. Behind her, Ivan commented, "That's very good. I suppose social historians are taught to dance quaint Japanese dances before they begin to write books?"

She ignored the teasing tone of his voice. "No, and I'm glad," she said. "I really do want to learn so much. It's easy to visualize the town, now, with the tired miners carrying their picks on their shoulders. I can see the big white moon hanging over the tall chimneys . . ."

Now when he spoke, there was something different in his voice. "You have the picture exactly. Strange . . ." He was silent for a moment, and then added, "Strange that you see what I felt myself! Once, when I was a boy, I went to visit a mining town at night. The land looked tired, and the moon was full. I wished I had a camera with me, but it wouldn't have caught the mood. There was a rough poetry there . . ."

A familiar nasal voice now interrupted. "Ivan Akira, you bad man! I have been trying to pin you down for the last fifteen minutes to ask you a question, and here you are talking to the pretty professor." Babette Lane fluttered her eyelashes. "Where is Miss Catherina da Silva tonight, I'd like to know?"

"In Hokkaido, with her father." Ivan's cool, amused mask had slipped back into place. "Was that the question you wanted to ask me? Now, if you ladies will excuse me . . ."

He nodded to them, moved away to his other guests. Babette Lane drew Rea out of the line of dancers.

"Fascinating man, isn't he?" she drawled. "Not at all what you would expect of a Japanese businessman." She nodded confidentially. "You know, the man is too damned sexy. If I were Catherina, I'd lock him up and throw away the key."

Rea glanced towards Ivan and found that he was watching her. Even though he was talking to his other guests, those green eyes kept seeking her out. With an effort, she turned her attention to Babette.

"Catherina?" She enquired.

"Catherina da Silva . . . his fiancée. His *unofficial* fiancée. She's Eurasian, too, you know, and I guess that gives them something in common besides money. She'd like to make their engagement watertight, but . . . no one can get Ivan Akira to do anything until he's good and ready."

"I believe you." Rea smiled wryly. "So far, I haven't even bagged an interview with him. Not yet, anyway!"

- 3 -

DESPITE HER JET LAG, Rea forced herself to rise early the next morning. She stumbled to the bathroom, splashed water on her face and dressed. Then she arranged tape recorder, notebooks and typewriter on her bedside desk and sat down before them. Usually, when she began a project, she started by putting in long hours of research before writing. This one was different. "I have no time," Rea muttered, turning on her tape recorder. She listened to the voices of the guests at last night's dinner party, the strumming of the *shamisen,* the guests singing and dancing. She leaned her chin on her arms, thinking.

It would be interesting to link the businessmen and diplomats at the party—modern figures of power—with the old rituals of geisha, dance and feasting. She could perhaps begin with the sword ceremony, continue on to the party, then swing right into an interview with Ivan Akira . . . provided, of course, he gave her one! He'd been reluctant to commit himself, had teased her about her book and the photographs.

"My photographs!" she said out loud. "Of course! That's how I'll do it!" She picked up the roll of film she had finished last night. "I'll develop these and send him the proofs. But it'll take time. . . ."

A couple of days to develop, a couple more to enlarge the photographs. But maybe not! Tucker would know where there was a darkroom to be found, and people who could do a rush job. She could make her pitch for an interview again, and maybe not just an interview, either—perhaps she could even visit the Akira factory! The idea ignited her enthusiasm.

She was hard at work compiling the outline of her first chapter when Janet knocked on the door. "You're not working already? You should be resting!" She said the same thing when Rea asked Tucker about an available darkroom. "Surely you can afford to rest *one* day, Rea?"

"No," Rea said, "I can't." Her voice was flat, and her friends stared at her. Slowly, she stirred her coffee, a frown pulling her delicate eyebrows together, darkening her hazel eyes with worry. "Jan, by this time next month I have to have a first draft clear in my mind. I've got to get started."

Janet and Tucker exchanged an anxious look. "Honey," Tucker said, becoming "Uncle" Tucker, "you came here to rest. Now that you've got your job at Reece, we thought—"

"I do have my job, but I might not have it long unless I get this book written," Rea interrupted. "I need tenure, and I won't get it unless I can prove that I'm good in my field. It's not an easy field for a woman to be in, and there's plenty of competition, believe me!" Her hands had started to tremble, and she forced herself to speak calmly. "I don't want to spend the rest of my day coasting around, as I did right after the divorce. I did a lot of things, you know . . . subbed at high schools, bagged groceries, waitressed. I wouldn't want to go back to doing that sort of thing."

Janet squared her wiry shoulders. "Tucker, you make sure Rea gets her photographs," she said. "After all"—she smiled—"Japanese hospitality demands that we do everything to keep our friends happy."

The Wynns were certainly friends she could count on under any circumstances, Rea thought early that afternoon after picking up her photographs at the headquarters of *Far East Outlook*. She felt that Tucker's advice was right—convince the Akiras that she'd put their name throughout her book, and she'd have a foot in the door with them. As she let herself back into the Wynns' apartment, she was mentally composing a letter to Ivan Akira, but a note left near the telephone by Janet changed her strategy.

Rea's pulse raced as she read the hastily-scrawled message. "Ivan Akira telephoned, asking for you," it said. "He was disappointed to find you out, and said he'd call you later."

For a brief moment, she felt the touch of Ivan's hand on her arm, the intensity of his sea-green eyes meeting hers across the roomful of guests at the Kin-Bara last night. Then she marshaled her thoughts. Ivan had phoned her. This was better than she'd expected. He was interested in their talk last night... he probably wanted to discuss an interview for her book, perhaps wanted to follow up on those photos she'd told him about! Maybe he wanted her to send them to him right away.

But why *send* the prints, when she herself could take them to him at Akira Industries?

She called Tucker's office, and his secretary gave Rea the phone numbers and addresses of both Akira Industries and Ivan's Osaka home. "He lives there with his sister, Midori-san, you know," she added. "I hear it's a very beautiful place."

Rea immediately dialed Ivan's office number, but she was in for a disappointment—he was in Nagoya for the day. So... that was that. Rea sighed as she hung up the phone, then frowned as another thought occurred to her. She did have the address of Ivan's Osaka home. Supposing she took the photos there?

Common sense told her that sending a letter with the photos was the most sensible thing to do. Yet, if Japanese industry was anything like its American counterpart, this would take time! Time for the posted letter to arrive at Akira Industries, time for the red tape of bureaucracy before it was answered, and then, perhaps, nothing but a polite letter of thanks at the end. Rea set her shoulders resolutely and gathered her purse and photos together. After all, Ivan had been interested enough to telephone her about the photos, hadn't he? He would probably be happy to have them delivered to his door!

The taxi trip to the Akiras' home was a long one, long enough for some of Rea's courage to run dry. Suppose no one was home? Suppose Midori, Ivan's sister, whom she'd met last night, was busy? She should have telephoned first! Her anxiety, however, was soon lost in delight as the cab left the city and sped into the suburbs, driving down long, narrow one-way streets which were shaded by picturesque willows and pines. Here, the wooden fences of old homes appeared between the ubiquitous apartment buildings, and Rea caught glimpses of slate-gray roofs and carefully tended gardens.

Finally, the taxi stopped in front of a large gateway set in a gray stone wall. The wall was high, and the top of it lined with broken chips of glass . . . to discourage thieves, Rea decided. The gateway itself was like a Japanese house in miniature. It had a slate-and-wood roof which towered above a rather forbidding weathered wooden door. Rea paid the taxi but asked the man to wait. Perhaps Midori was not in, after all. She took a deep breath, set her shoulders, then walked to the door and rang the bell.

For a moment, nothing happened. Then she heard shuffling foorsteps coming towards the gate. "Who's there?" a querulous voice called in Japanese.

"My name is Rea Harley, and I would like to see Miss Akira—"

She broke off as the door creaked open, revealing a trace of wispy beard and suspicious narrow eyes. "I know no one by the name of Harley," the old man said. He pronounced it "Har-ree."

"No, you don't know me. I only wish to see Miss Akira."

"Does the *Ojosan,* the young lady of the house, know you?"

Rea shook her head reluctantly. The door closed with a bang. Rea could hear the man muttering something about mad foreigners and tourists. Behind her, the taxi driver snickered, and her cheeks became hot.

Before she realized what she was doing, she banged on the door. "Open up!" she called, and then stopped, horrified. The old man on the other side of the door seemed equally horrified. He called out something, and now other footsteps were running towards the gate. The door creaked open a second time, this time revealing the round, surprised face of a young woman.

"What is it that you require?" the young woman said politely. Rea ran through her speech a second time.

"I met Miss Akira last night at the Kin-Bara. I took some

photographs of the occasion and would like to present them to her if she has a moment to see me," she explained.

"Please wait a minute," the woman replied, and again, the door shut.

Rea didn't know whether to laugh, be offended, wait or go back in the cab and drive away. As she was debating, the door swung open, all the way, this time. Rea found herself looking into a courtyard tiled with tiny pebbles of all shapes and colors. The young woman bowed deeply.

"Dozo," she said. "Please come in."

Rea dismissed the waiting cab and followed the bowing maid. As she looked around her at the traditional home and fine-sanded Japanese garden surrounding it, she couldn't help taking in her breath with pleasure. From where she stood, Rea could see a stone lantern half hidden by carefully rounded shrubs. A pool full of water lilies was shaded by a small thicket of bamboo, which rustled in the breeze.

"Ojosan is in a farther garden," the maid explained deferentially. "Please to come this way."

She led Rea through the rounded shrubs, past the stone lantern and through a low gate made of bamboo. Now they walked on sand so soft and fine that Rea had the urge to kick off her shoes and go barefoot. In this garden, shaded by pine and maple and scented with roses, was a small table, at which two young women were seated, conversing. As Rea approached, they stopped talking to look at her, and one got to her feet. Rea recognized the pretty woman who had worn the yellow kimono at the Kin-Bara restaurant last night.

Today, Midori wore a light cotton dress and spoke in barely accented English. "How do you do? I'm Midori Akira. My maid says you have met me, but I am not sure I remember. . . ." The young woman was friendly. "She mangled your name so badly, I am not even sure what it is."

Rea responded to the warmth in Midori's eyes. She introduced herself, explained her errand and was relieved to see that her smile widened into a grin.

"But now I *do* remember you! You danced the *tankobushi* with my brother, and did it very well." She took Rea's hand and drew her towards the table and chairs. "Come and sit down, Miss Harley, and meet Catherina da Silva."

Catherina da Silva! Rea tried not to stare or show surprise as the other young woman rose. Taller than Midori, Catherina showed touches of her Western heritage in the heavy-lidded dark eyes, the cut of her imperious nose. However, she looked much more like a slim, beautiful aristocratic Japanese than a European, and Rea remembered what Babette Lane had said about Catherina being Eurasian. After all, she reminded herself, the Portuguese had been among the first Westerners to come to Japan, and there probably had been much intermarriage in spite of objections from strict Japanese families. She murmured a greeting as the beautiful, well-dressed young woman held out a bejewelled hand.

"Miss Harley," Catherina drawled. "You are a photographer for *Far East Outlook* magazine?" Rea explained that she was a friend of the Wynns', in Japan to write a book. Catherina seated herself, brushing an imaginary dust mote from her immaculate sleeve. The diamonds on her fingers flashed in the sunlight. "And you are writing a book about Japan?" she asked.

Rea plunged into explanations. After all, this was what she had come for . . . to ask for a chance to see Akira Industries. Catherina looked bored, but Midori seemed genuinely interested.

"I think it's a fine idea. I wish I was clever enough to write a book on social history." She took Rea's photographs and spread them out on the table before her. "These are marvelous! I will be sure to show them to my brother, and I know he'll let you interview him."

"Your brother is a busy man," Catherina rebuked Midori. "You shouldn't promise anything in his name." She rose, graceful and elegant, and Rea had the distinct impression Catherina was looking down her aristocratic nose at the gauche American who wanted to write a book. "I will see you and Ivan at supper, then, Midori?"

Midori got up to say her goodbyes, and after a nod at Rea, Catherina strolled away through the garden. Rea watched her ruefully, then turned as Midori chuckled.

"She doesn't mean anything personal," Midori said. "Catherina is very *royal*. Sometimes I call her Queen Catherine to her face." She sat down again, wriggling comfortably. "Now, please tell me more about your book . . . may I call you Rea?"

"Oh, please do!" Rea warmed even more to Midori. "I hope I haven't been rude, coming here this way," she said. "I really did want you to have the photographs and to ask my favor."

"The book is so important?" Midori asked sympathetically. Rea nodded. "I was never very good at history," the petite woman went on, "but I remember a lesson that was drummed into our heads about the Japanese character's being based on diligence, self-denial and loyalty. Is that the kind of thing you are going to write about?"

"Exactly!" Rea leaned forward eagerly. "Those characteristics all come from Zen Buddhism. Nowadays, the modern factory worker uses those same qualities in his work. I need to see modern industry at work so I can tie the past and the present together."

She forgot herself as she poured out her ideas. Halfway through a sentence, however, she stopped, dismayed that she might have bored Midori who was listening carefully. "I talk too much," Rea said contritely. "You should have stopped me."

"No, I like to hear you talk." Midori grinned. "Of course, I didn't understand many of the difficult words you used. My father insisted I learn English, but I don't speak it half as well as Ivan." She clapped her hands. "I have an idea. Stay for lunch and tell me more."

Rea was delighted to accept. Over lunch—a cold vegetable soup laced with sherry and lemon, sandwiches and fruit—Midori asked questions in both Japanese and English. As she answered queries about American women, fashions and society abroad, Rea realized that although Midori gave the appearance of being very modern, she had been much sheltered.

Midori herself said this was true. "My father had me educated," she said with a sigh. "However, I am considered ornamental by the men of my family. Eventually, I suppose I will get married. It must be wonderful to do important work, as you are, Rea."

"You could do anything you wanted to," Rea said gently, and Midori threw up her small hands, laughing.

"I know, I know! At heart, I am terribly lazy. I like being waited on and catered to . . . so I don't rebel against the restrictions put on me. After all, we are in Japan. Up to very recently, men were considered all-powerful in this country."

Rea had a sudden, vivid picture of tall, commanding Ivan Akira, his green eyes challenging and mocking hers. She frowned. Powerful, she thought, rich . . . his every whim attended to. She didn't care for the Japanese concept of men and women.

After a long visit, Rea said goodbye. She was sorry to leave Midori, and protested when she insisted that Rea be driven back to the Wynns' in the family car. Rea arrived at the Wynns' in state, chauffeured by a respectful old gentleman. Unfortunately, neither Tucker nor Janet was home to witness this triumphant return.

Instead, a note greeted her. "Dinner is in the fridge. . . . I have an emergency at the clinic, and Tucker has an awful cocktail party to cover for the magazine." Janet added that she hoped Rea's day had gone well.

Rea showered, then changed into jeans and a T-shirt. After pulling her hair back into a ponytail, she took her tape recorder, notes and photos to the couch beneath the living-room window. She had meant to work, but the sight of twilight sweeping down over Osaka made her forget. She hadn't even turned on the light, when someone rang the doorbell.

She hurried to the door, then hesitated, mindful of the tall gates and glass-topped walls she had seen that day. "Who's there?"

"Akira." His voice was imperious. Surprised, and rather concerned about how she must look, she opened the door. He came in at once. He was dressed for evening, in an immaculate white linen suit, which made her feel even more acutely conscious of her casual appearance, in ponytail and jeans.

"I'm very sorry, the Wynns aren't here right now," she began. He looked at her without a smile, his handsome features expressionless. "Won't you sit down?"

"No. I have a dinner engagement and can't stay." There was a fractional pause. "You visited my sister today."

So that was why he'd come! Pleasure welled up in her as she realized he was going to give her an interview. "I developed the photographs today," she began.

"Why didn't you mail them?" His eyes were as hard as jade, and she suddenly realized how angry his voice was. Standing so close to him, she felt the tension that seemed to crackle from him. Involuntarily, she took a step backward.

"I . . . I heard that you'd telephoned me, and assumed that you wanted the photographs quickly," she said, trying to speak reasonably in spite of the tension within her. "I wanted to—"

"I know what you wanted to do! You wanted to use a young girl's sympathies in order to get what you wanted. You wanted an interview with me, and you wanted to see how modern-day aristocrats live. I imagine you consider all this enterprising, but I consider your manners, as you Americans would put it, cheap."

His words were like a slap in the face. Rea felt her cheeks flame as she fought for control. "Look, I'm sorry if I offended you. Your phone call . . . I thought it was about the photographs, my book!"

"Your *book!*" Rea had never heard so much contempt packed into two words. "My phone call had nothing to do with your book. I merely wanted to see you . . ." he might have said more, but Rea was furious herself, now. She clenched her small fists at her side and tried to keep her voice from quivering with anger.

"Yes, my book! I don't have much time to write it, which is why I went to see your sister. It's important to me to—"

He cut her short. "Privacy is important to the Japanese. You ought to know that if you're any kind of social historian! And though I'm broad-minded about many things, I will not tolerate anyone's using my sister or my family in any way." He took a step closer, diminishing the already small distance between them. It took all her control to stand firm. What had Tucker said about Ivan Akira? That under the façade of his cool mockery lay a ruthless mind? Involuntarily, her foot moved backward, catching against the grass matting. She stumbled.

He reached out a hand to steady her, and she felt the strength of his clasp. "Be careful," he said mockingly. "You wouldn't want to fall on your face, would you? Or is this another ruse to get that precious interview from me?" He didn't let go of her, but pulled her closer, the closeness a menacing one, from which she could not free herself. "I suppose in America this sort of thing goes on all the time," he continued. "Big-corporation heads are susceptible to those wide golden eyes of yours and to your seductive body. I would imagine you get very good results."

"If you think I went to . . . to . . . Take your hands off me!" she cried.

"Why? It would spoil the effect. I'm sorry I'm not in the market, at the moment, for those who trade sex for favors, but it was a good try."

His hands left her arms, traveled up to cup her face and tilt her head backward. Then, moving deliberately, he pulled her against him and brought his mouth down on hers. The touch of his lips on hers filled her with a shock of panic . . . panic for the whirl of sudden desire that left her giddy and defenseless against his mouth and lips and bold, probing tongue. She could taste him, smell the scent of his after-shave, feel the strength of his tall, powerful body pressed against hers. She could hardly breathe, barely think.

It didn't seem important to think. Then he stepped away from her, but still held her face in the palms of his hands. For a second, there was silence between them; then he said, "It's really too bad. Your . . . er . . . technique is excellent. I am sure you'll get all the interviews you want."

She pulled loose from him, fury boiling up inside her. "Get out of here!" she whispered coldly.

"You don't want to interview me?" It was too dark to see his face, but she knew his green eyes were mocking her. She hated him.

"I don't ever want to see you again. . . ." she gasped, then heard him laugh softly as he turned toward the door.

"Good night, professor," he said, then he closed the door very quietly between them.

- 4 -

REA'S FIRST ACT was to turn on the lights. Darkness made her feel too alone, too vulnerable to the sensations that were still racking her body. Shivering, she wrapped her arms around herself in a hugging motion, one she always used when she felt insecure. She still felt Ivan's closeness, the sensation of that powerful male body pressed against hers. He'd humiliated her . . . and she'd let him use her own body to accomplish the humiliation! She was suddenly grateful for the anger that now boiled through her, because it almost canceled out the horrible aloneness.

But it didn't completely go away. That was the trouble with strong emotions, Rea though unhappily. She felt raw and in pain. These last few months, she had been numb. She had felt that when Bill left, he had taken all feelings with him. But now, here was the spurting of her desire, the aching fullness that clung to her breasts, the heaviness in her loins. All this told her her body was still alive, and achingly eager. But . . . for Ivan Akira?

She didn't sleep well, partly from jet lag, partly because of the dreams that kept her from falling into a deep sleep. At six, she got up, showered and, ignoring Janet's pleas to "sleep in," began jotting down telephone numbers. Tucker had a typewritten sheet of all the main business offices in Japan, and now that she'd accepted the fact that she wouldn't be able to study Akira Industries, she called each one, explaining her purpose and asking for interviews. Many of the firms seemed hesitant, but a few agreed, and she made appointments with two managers of large companies. She had just finished talking to a publicity rep from Tanaka Textiles when the phone rang.

Thinking it must be a return call from one of the firms

she'd contacted, Rea snapped up the receiver and answered crisply. The voice at the other end of the line was equally clipped. "Rea Harley?" Ivan said. "Akira here."

She was tempted to hang up on him but realized that would be childish and stupid. "Yes," she said curtly. "How can I help you?"

"I believe the shoe's on the other foot, professor. The question is, what can I do for *you?*" There was a short pause, during which Rea again felt like hanging up. Then he said, "My father, the baron, feels that Akira Industries should give you every assistance in researching your book. I am at the Osaka office today and could begin showing you around, if that's convenient."

Rea's head felt as if it was spinning. "You mean . . . you're going to help me? Now?"

"If it's convenient." In spite of his smooth tone, she realized that it was *not* convenient for him. She sensed an undercurrent of hostility below his courteous words. "I'll send the office car for you. Can you be ready in half an hour?"

"Of—of course," she stammered. "I want to thank—"

He cut her short. "Please inform the receptionist when you arrive at the office. I will be seeing you in a short while, then." The phone clicked in her ear.

Rea had always moved quickly. Today, however, was the exception. Half an hour was plenty of time to get ready, but she skittered with indecision. She was impatient with herself as she tried to decide which of her two good blouses to wear with her business suit. The navy-blue silk one was dressy but it looked too hot, whereas the mauve blouse had an open neck and might not be the thing to wear for her first interview. And then there was her hair. Should she wear it down, around her face, or in a chignon? Finally, she decided that the chignon gave her a professional look. She had to win Ivan's respect.

Her hands were shaking when she carried all her paraphernalia downstairs and got into the official, dark-blue car from Ivan's office. Mercifully, it was air-conditioned, but she could see the heat shimmering on the sidewalks and on the long stretch of Mido-suji road before her. As they turned into the busy Honmachi business district, the chauffeur began pointing out various office buildings. That one was owned by an American firm, he said. Over there was Jinno Electronics.

"And there is Akira Industries," he added with obvious pride.

Rea found that she was impressed by the building, which somehow stood out from the rest. Imposing, with large glass doors and tiers of windows, it conveyed a beauty of design that the other office buildings lacked.

"The company president, the baron, built this five years ago," the chauffeur told her. He pronounced the name of the baron with reverence. "The young vice-president designed the building."

"You mean Mr. Ivan Akira was the architect?" Rea asked, surprised. She leaned back in the car to look at the building again, noting its grace and elegance. Tucker hadn't told her that the man had this kind of talent!

She wondered still more when she left the car and walked through the sliding doors into a red-carpeted foyer, where a receptionist sat behind a desk. Rea introduced herself, and the receptionist got up and bowed many times.

"*Hai*. Yes, Miss Rea Harley . . . please wait a moment!" She indicated a comfortable red leather chair some distance from the desk. "I will tell the vice-president that you are here."

Rea looked around at the reception room. Had Ivan designed the interior of the office as well? She noted with pleasure his use of space and lighting, the texture of rug and wallpaper.

"Have you been waiting long?"

Ivan had approached so soundlessly, she hadn't heard him. She rose in some confusion. "I was admiring your handiwork." She nodded to the room around her. "I didn't know you were an architect."

"My father let me amuse myself," he replied, reserve in his voice. He continued, "Will you come up to my office? I've asked some journalists to meet there. They'll take some photographs. I'll explain what we are trying to do, on the way up."

Ivan gestured Rea into the elevator, and as she passed him, his hand brushed her arm. Even through the sleeve of her suit, his touch generated the same electricity she'd felt the night before. Rea felt her cheeks growing hot and quickly glanced at Ivan. He was staring ahead, his mouth tight and his eyes cold.

"My father and I had a long telephone conversation this morning," he said. "It seems that my younger sister told him about you. As a result, he feels that you would benefit Akira Industries by being affiliated with us. In return for any help you could give us, we'd introduce you as our protégée to presidents of major companies and so on."

Rea was stunned. "I'll do everything I possibly can," she said, "but to be honest, I don't know that my book will bring you so much publicity. Of course, I'd give you credit and talk about you, but. . . but it's not likely to be a runaway best-seller or anything like that. It's most likely to be read by university people."

Ivan shrugged. "My father is interested in publicity, yes, but that's not his main reason for wanting your help," he said. "Let me explain. We have a very important business contact coming to Japan for a brief stay. His name is Jim Hume, and he will be in the Osaka area a week or so from now." The green eyes looked down on her without a hint of mockery, and she remembered Tucker's remarks about Ivan's acute business brain. "He represents a company with whom Akira Industries very deeply desires business contacts."

"But how could I—"

He interrupted her. "Jim Hume is a history buff. He has always wanted to write a history of Japan but has never had the courage to start this project. My father thinks that if Hume talks to you, realizes you are writing a book also, finds you a kindred spirit. . ."

"I would encourage him in his project and. . . and he'd feel grateful to you," Rea murmured. "I don't know whether it would work."

His smile was cynical. "You are a professor, aren't you? It's your job to inspire lagging students! The question, of course, is whether you have enough confidence in your abilities to work with us."

The elevator stopped, and the doors slid smoothly open. Ivan's eyebrows quirked up, and once again she read challenge in the clear green eyes. "Well, professor?" he asked.

"I... yes. Of course. I'll do anything I can to help."

"Good." He bowed, ushering her out with a princely air. Rea walked before him up a carpeted hallway, then to a large reception area filled with reporters. Someone from *Outlook* was there, as was Babette Lane. Rea paused on the threshold and looked back at Ivan questioningly.

"We'll have them in my office, I think," he told her. "It's the door over there... just beyond the reception area. After you, professor."

The mockery was back in his eyes and voice, and made her square her shoulders and lift her head as she made her way through the throng of press. Feeling as if she were about to give a lecture to a difficult class, she preceded Ivan through the doorway and into the room beyond.

"This way... I'm sorry we've kept you waiting, but there'll be time for photos and questions," she heard Ivan telling the press. He spoke genially, but there was an unmistakable ring of authority in his voice. Though she disliked the man heartily, Rea had to admire the deft way he handled the press as they all entered the large, sumptuously decorated office. Rea had a confused impression of pale-green carpets, white walls hung with artwork, an enormous rosewood desk set against picture windows that looked out on the city. After a picture-taking session, Ivan read a prepared statement about cooperation between industry and education. She admired the smooth way in which he correlated the two, wondered who wrote his material... then realized he probably did it himself.

The reporters asked questions after the statement was read. Why was Rea so interested in Japan? How well could she speak the language? How did she feel about America's stand on trade... labor... defense? Ivan finally interposed.

"Any further questions will have to be answered in the professor's book," he joked, and there was scattered laughter. "Any final questions?"

It seemed that everyone's curiosity was satiated—except Babette Lane's. As the press filed out, she reached over and grabbed Rea by the elbow, leaning close. "Will you tell me how you got that gorgeous man to let you interview him?" she purred, and one well-made-up eye winked. "And I thought professors were shy intellectuals."

She thinks I'm sleeping with him, Rea thought, glaring after the departing reporter. Her irritation increased as she realized Ivan had heard every word. He was watching her with a cynical expression.

"You mustn't be concerned with what the reporters think," he said urbanely. "She can hardly print her suspicions about us in the *Daily!*"

Rea felt her cheeks grow hot, and to cover her confusion, studied the art on the walls. To make things worse, the first picture she saw was one of Picasso's nudes. "I admire the genius of the man," Ivan said coolly, behind her. "Perhaps you'd like to see more of his . . . er . . . amorous work?"

He was baiting her. Remembering the power of his arms and the feel of his mouth on hers, Rea bit her lip. He had made no move to touch or even come close to her, but she felt a strange tension in her body. She turned and saw him flick his eyes over her, her reddened face, her breasts. He smiled. "Perhaps," he murmured, "my father's orders will be a pleasure to carry out. . . ."

Almost desperately, she turned her attention from the Picasso nude to a large scroll of Japanese calligraphy. "Is this a Nando?"

"You know Nando's work?" He sounded astonished.

"Not well," she admitted, "but the Wynns have a scroll by him, and I thought I recognized the brush strokes." She stepped back to admire the magnificent scroll. "I'm not very good with written Japanese, I'm afraid. Does it say something about summer?"

"A haiku by Shiki," he said abruptly. "Roughly, it translates to, 'Long the summer days, patterns on the ocean sand . . . our idle footprints.'"

Rea stood for a long moment, absorbing the bold yet delicate characters. "Summer days aren't long," she murmured, "and the tide does wash away our footprints. . . ." She turned and saw that he was watching her with a strange expression in his sea-green eyes. "Since the days *are* short, I'd better get to work," she said.

"Certainly. I suggest you follow this itinerary." He

walked to the rosewood desk and flipped open a pad. "Today, you'll meet with our employees here. Tomorrow, I suggest a meeting with the president of a company called Kingo. That's a good glass company, and it's usually eager for publicity. There will be trips to Nagoya, Kobe . . . and perhaps a meeting with Inada, the big owner of a private TV station. A TV spot would impress the people at Reece, wouldn't it?"

She nodded, a little dazed. He smiled his old mocking smile as he moved to usher her out of the office. "If you come here early tomorrow morning," he went on, "you'll be in time to hear our employees sing the company song." She looked questioningly at him. "Oh, yes, we have a company song. It is all about diligence and honesty and progress, and is sung by all our employees each morning. Paternalism, I think you social historians call it."

He swept her down the carpeted hallway and into the elevator, and they descended to a lower floor. Here, Rea stepped into a large room that looked like a one-room office. There were no cubicles or dividers separating desk from desk. Again Ivan explained. "Our employees aren't separated into different offices for a reason. They like to see one another as they work."

Rea looked around her, noting the neatly suited men, the women in dark skirts and white blouses. On the wall facing them was a huge, framed photograph of a tall, slender man with dark hair and a faint mustache.

"The baron, my father," Ivan said.

As if these words were some kind of signal, an older man seated at a far desk jumped to his feet. He called out an order, and Rea blinked as all the office workers got to their feet in unison and began to exercise. The older man led the calesthenics, bending to the right, the left, the center.

"One, two three . . . *ichi, ni, san* . . ." he chanted.

"Want to try it?" Ivan smiled down at Rea. "It's a good way to stretch the muscles and break up the day. That man leading the pack is Satoh-san. He's our department manager on this floor."

When the calesthenics were over, Ivan led Rea among the employees. She questioned them, and they shyly but willingly answered her questions. One young man said he was twenty-six, and had joined the company last year, right after graduating from Osaka University. Now that he was a "salary man," his loyalty to Akira Industries was deep and fervent.

Rea had been prepared for a deep-seated loyalty to the company, but she was surprised at the depth of feeling the employees had for their employer and his firm. It seemed that the employees depended on the company for more than just a salary. They lived on company-held land, went to resorts that gave cut rates to companies, played company-sponsored sports. Some even used the company computer to find dates.

Rea questioned some of the women as well as the men and found that many Japanese wives worked after their marriage, in order to keep up with the cost of living. However, there was a disparity. "Up to very recently, Japanese women found it distasteful to work," Ivan explained. "Even now, the man is considered the breadwinner. If a job opens, and a man and woman with equal qualifications apply for the job, the man gets it every time."

"So men are still all-powerful in Japan," Rea murmured. He raised his eyebrows.

"Is that a statement or a judgment, professor?"

Before she could answer, Satoh-san, the little man who'd led the calesthenics, came running over. He looked distressed. "Akira-san, there's been a phone call from Osaka Hospital." He paused. "It's the Kimura family. Their daughter has been in a very bad accident."

He plunged into rapid Japanese, and Rea saw Ivan's face turn grave and worried as he heard about the six-year-old Kimura girl who had been hit by a speeding car. It was feared that she had brain damage, and the mother was hysterical. He turned to Rea, his eyes full of concern.

"I'm sorry, but I'll have to go to the hospital at once. The head of the household is one of our employees, away in Hong Kong on business. I'm sorry about today, but Satoh-san will—"

She interrupted. "Can I come with you to the hospital?" His eyebrows rose, and she hastened to explain. "I promise not to say a word, or get in the way or do anything to bother you."

"I think that a family crisis is hardly the time for research. But . . . you can come, I suppose." He spoke impatiently, irritably. "We'll take the car. It's waiting for us in front."

He hurried her into the elevator and then out of the office building. She glanced at his tense face, wishing she could ask a question but not daring. They had ridden several miles before he turned to her with a faintly apologetic smile.

"It must seem melodramatic to you, but this sort of thing happens often. The head of the company is responsible for his employees . . . and their families. And you heard Satoh-san. The wife is hysterical."

She nodded. "I knew that the head of a company was like the head of a big family. You yourself called it paternalism. But I didn't realize how much to heart you took all of this."

"Well, paternalism is a big word. A vague concept. Michiko Kimura is a little girl. Out playing on the street for a second . . . and then the accident. The wife has no relatives living in Osaka, and she has many younger children." He paused. "I've asked Satoh to reach Dr. Matsui in Tokyo. He's the best brain-man in Japan. I'm having him flown in for a consultation."

Rea looked at Ivan in surprise, then gave herself a mental shake. Ivan Akira was an industrial giant, and he had power . . . and more money than she'd ever dreamed of! She was suddenly glad for the power and the money which would buy little Michiko Kimura a chance at life. She thought of the hurt child and found that she had unconsciously wrapped her arms around herself in that vague, vulnerable gesture again. Ivan glanced down at her and smiled briefly, as if realizing her concern.

"I am sure it is going to be all right. Ah . . . here is Osaka Hospital."

They were immediately escorted to a waiting room where a red-eyed young woman sat surrounded by three frightened little children. Two of them clung to their mother, and the third, a chubby little boy of about eighteen months, was wailing and rubbing his knuckles into swollen eyes. When Ivan entered the room, the mother leaped to her feet and, shaking off her children, ran to him. Rea saw him bend to take her hands and speak gently but firmly to her.

"You must be strong and sensible for your child's sake," she heard him say. "Look, I am here. You must not worry. Leave things to me."

Rea turned to the children. How to distract them? Then she had it—her tape recorder. "Do you want to hear your own voices?" she asked softly in Japanese. The children stared at her. She pulled out the machine and pressed a button. The little boy gave a loud wail at this moment, and one of the other children cried his name. Rea played back this exchange, and the children stared, amazed.

"Aunty, how did you do that?" one youngster asked. They crowded close.

Ivan now came up to Rea. "I'm going with Mrs. Kimura for a moment to talk to the doctors. Can you take care of the children till then?" He was hesitant, but she nodded quickly.

"Of course I can. I'm glad to be able to do something. Just do whatever is necessary for the little girl."

He hesitated, then nodded, and walked away with the mother. The children hardly saw her go, for they were all busily talking into the tape. After a while, Rea got them to sing folk songs, many of which she had heard on tapes back in Boston. They were all still singing together when Ivan returned.

This time he was alone. "The child's condition has stabilized, so things are looking up," he told Rea. "I'm going to send Mrs. Kimura and her youngsters home in the office car. She can't do anything here, and I've promised to stay at the hospital till Dr. Matsui arrives." He paused, shaking his head. "You seem to have had your hands full."

"I've enjoyed it." Rea snuggled the littlest boy closer to her, then let him go. The older children said their suddenly shy goodbyes.

"As soon as the office car returns from the Kimuras, I'll have him drive you home," Ivan went on. "Or, if you prefer, I'll call a taxi for you now."

"Don't worry about me. Besides . . . while waiting, I can ask you some questions."

He laughed. "You never give up, do you?" he asked, but for once, there was no hostility in his voice. Then, gathering the children together, he walked away from her. Rea watched as the tall figure surrounded by small ones moved down the hall, then found herself smiling as Ivan reached down to lift the smallest into his arms and onto his broad shoulder. He was easy with the children, relaxed . . . different. Another facet of Ivan Akira, she thought. As the elevator closed on them all, she began to play back the songs she and the children had sung together.

"Good heavens, Miss Harley . . . what a surprise. What are you doing here?"

Rea turned sharply at the familiar drawling voice. Catherina da Silva was walking towards her.

- 5 -

AS USUAL, REA NOTED, Catherina was dressed in the height of fashion. Feeling very conscious of her plain navy blouse and suit, now wrinkled a little from holding the littlest Kimura boy, Rea got to her feet.

"Surely you aren't ill?" Catherina asked, barely touching Rea's outstretched hand with her fingertips.

"No, nothing like that. I was interviewing Mr. Akira, and then one of his employees' children was hurt. It was an emergency." Rea's voice trailed off as she realized Catherina's attention had switched to Ivan, who was walking down the room towards them.

"Catherina!" Ivan's smile was surprised. "What are you doing here?"

"Visiting duty," Catherina said, and made a wry little face. "One of Father's employees had a baby, so I came to see her and the child. I heard that you were here, so I came down to see why."

"The Kimura girl was hit by a car. Some truck driver went out of control. The roads are narrow, and they drive so fast," Ivan said.

Rea realized that they'd forgotten about her. Catherina had turned her back towards her, as if she meant to completely cut her out of the conversation.

"You sent the Kimuras home in your car, I suppose. Do you need a lift back to your office? I've got my car here," Catherina was saying. "I have to ask your advice anyway, Ivan. It's about that summer house Father wants to build in Matsumoto. The blueprints just came in, and I'm not satisfied. I wish you'd look at them."

Ivan suddenly seemed to realize that Rea was standing there.

"I've promised Miss Harley, here, an interview," he said. "Besides, I've got to wait for Dr. Matsui."

Catherina glanced at Rea, her eyebrows arching. "But surely Miss Harley won't mind. As for Dr. Matsui, he won't be here for hours. At least walk to the car with me and look over the blueprints."

Ivan hesitated, and Rea knew what was expected of her. "It's perfectly all right," she said quickly. "We can continue our discussion tomorrow." She half expected Ivan to say that there was no inconvenience in talking here and now, but Catherina had already slid an arm through his.

"I'll send the office car for you at eight-thirty," Ivan now said. "Kingo Glass, remember . . . and the company song."

"Yes, of course. Thank you." Rea watched them walk away, and felt a strange disappointment. He hadn't even asked if she needed a taxi home to the Wynns'. But then . . . why should he? None of this had been Ivan's idea. His father was the one convinced that she would be an asset to the firm. To Ivan, she was only a pest, a nuisance who was writing some silly book.

She took a taxi back to the Wynns', a taxi that cost so much that she vowed to investigate the city's bus routes. Osaka seemed so complicated . . . but after all, she'd only been in Japan forty-eight-odd hours, and she was probably still suffering from jet lag. That had to be the reason why she felt so tired and dispirited. There was no reason to feel as she did, after all. She'd accomplished a great deal.

Carrying her tape recorder to the window in the living room, she sank down onto the couch and pressed the "play" button. Then she smiled, as the room filled with children's voices singing folk songs. She leaned her face on her arm, closing her eyes, listening to the sweet treble voices. Suddenly, Ivan Akira's voice interrupted the sing-along. His dep tones came so suddenly, so unexpectedly, that she gasped. She'd forgotten that he had interrupted her while she was taping songs with the children. . . .

"Hello, you alone? I thought I heard voices." Jan Wynn was just coming in, and she looked at Rea in surprise. Rea shut off the tape recorder, and Janet added, "It's my half day at the clinic. I came home to see if you were resting and whether you felt up to shopping or seeing the sights or . . . whatever."

"I've just gotten home myself." Rea gave her friend a description of the morning's activities, and Janet's eyes widened.

"That's terrific!" She exclaimed, plopping down beside Rea on the couch. "The Akiras will be able to open all kinds of doors for you. . . ." Then she frowned. "If you were with Ivan Akira, how come the children's voices?"

Rea explained about the hospital. "So you ended up baby-sitting." Janet grinned. "You were always good with kids, Rea. I always wondered why you never had any of your own."

"Bill didn't think it was the right time to start a family," Rea answered. "We argued about it a lot at first, but Bill convinced me it was the right thing for us both."

Janet ran a hand through her cap of gray curls. "Bill always managed to talk you into doing things his way, didn't he?" she said wrathfully. "That man! Convincing you to give up your career. If you hadn't left Reece when you married him, you'd be a full professor by now, wouldn't you? None of this worry, this 'publish or perish' stuff. You'd be established."

Rea shook her head. Usually, she didn't want to think, let alone talk about Bill Delahey. But today, she found she could look back over the years with Bill and feel almost no pain.

"No use blaming Bill for everything, Jan. I was to blame, too. I was in love with him, you know." She paused, her eyes looking back over the long years. "I was only twenty-four when we met . . . and he was so handsome and talented and smart. At the time, I thought that if I didn't have Bill, my life wasn't worth living." A sad smile curved her lips for a moment. "Giving up my job at Reece didn't seem like any kind of sacrifice, not when I could be Bill Delahey's wife."

Janet kicked off her shoes, curling up on the couch. "But why did he insist you give up your job? Lots of women marry and keep on working. Look at Tucker and me!"

"Most women don't marry freelance photographers,"

Rea pointed out. "Besides, Tucker's always been proud of your career, Jan. Bill didn't want a 'professional' wife. We talked it all over, and he convinced me that being a professor at Reece was a boring job. He said that we had to be ready to move around the country at a moment's notice because of his job, and that he wanted me to be with him. I guess he really did want me there . . . at first, anyway."

And they had traveled. Baja, New Orleans, Mexico, Peru . . . She wrapped her arms around herself unconsciously, then spoke again. "Sounds exciting, huh? It wasn't, you know. After a while it was just third-rate hotel rooms and horrible weather and getting sick in places where there was no doctor. Once, I got pneumonia out in some mountain village in the Yucatan . . . and then there was the time Bill ran a raging fever out in Baja and I had to tramp miles to try to get help for him."

"And yet, he left you."

Janet's voice was tight with anger. Her eyes snapped as Rea nodded.

"He said that we weren't being fair to each other. Maybe he was right. In a few years, we'd have split up anyway, and where would I be? At least, I lucked out. Reece had an opening and took me back."

There was a little silence, and Rea heard, far in the distance somewhere, a child singing an old Japanese folk song—one of the songs the Kimura children had sung to her in the hospital.

"Was it hard?" Janet asked gently. "After the divorce, I mean. Before Reece took you back."

Rea thought of the year after the divorce . . . going to interviews, agonizing afterward: Did they like me? Will they hire me? She thought of packing supermarket bags, working in a camera shop, waitressing, factory work, subbing in the local schools.

"I was lucky," she said out loud. "The trouble is . . . now that Reece *has* taken me back, I'm terrified of losing my job. You know how hard it is in education, these days. I really need to make this book good, Jan. That's why it's wonderful that the Akiras are taking me on board like this."

Janet snorted. "Don't you waste too much time being grateful to that lot," she said. "They wouldn't do anything for nothing. You watch out for this Jim Hume they want you to butter up for them!"

Rea laughed. "Jan, stop being a mother hen. I'm thirty-one not twenty-four, and there's no more razzle-dazzle in my life." She stopped for a moment, remembering the way Catherina had linked her arm through Ivan's. For some reason, the memory hurt. "That's the way I want it," she ended firmly.

Next morning, Rea was at Akira Industries early, so that she could hear the company song being sung. As the song about diligence and loyalty swelled from so many throats, Rea watched the faces in fascination.

"Are you enjoying this?" Ivan whispered, behind her. She turned and saw him regarding her with his usual expression of barely concealed mockery. "I doubt whether GM or Chrysler or any of your big American companies command this kind of devotion," he continued.

"Perhaps not. But then, how many vice-presidents of companies would do what you did for the Kimura girl? How is Michiko this morning?"

Ivan's face softened momentarily, and the green eyes were genuinely glad as he nodded. "Better, thank heavens. Dr. Matsui found no evidence of brain damage, so she didn't even need surgery. She's resting comfortably right now, and the doctors are observing her. So is her father. I had him flown back from Hong Kong immediately, of course." He paused. "I have a message from the mother, by the way. For you."

Rea was surprised. "A message for me?"

"She said that you had a gentle heart, to do what you did for her children yesterday. They couldn't stop talking about the nice foreign aunty who could sing Japanese folk songs." His voice turned dry. "Part of your training, no doubt, professor."

She matched his tone. "Of course. Now, today, you spoke about a visit to the Kingo Glass factory?"

"The appointment is set for ten o'clock. We do some business with the Kingo people, so they're only too happy to do us a favor and answer the questions of the learned American professor."

His sarcasm was so obvious this time that she bit her lip. All she said, however, was, "Please don't call me a professor. I'm only an assistant professor. There's a world of difference between the two."

"It's hard to believe that a determined young woman hasn't been promoted by now," he said. The words should have been a compliment, but Rea knew they were a veiled insult. She felt her cheeks burn as he continued, "I'm sure that there were many ways in which you could have ensured yourself a promotion."

She controlled herself and did not answer, and was relieved when he said, "The car is waiting to take us to Kingo Glass." Then, as they walked towards the elevator, he added, "Since you and I are going to be together for some days, I feel as if Akira Industries should have some knowledge of your personal history. You won't mind if I ask some questions?"

Of course I mind, Rea thought angrily. She controlled herself, however, and nodded. "Please ask your questions, Mr. Akira."

"You see, the presidents of the companies we visit are busy men. Occasionally, they need to know a little about you before they agree to see you. For instance, they might ask why, after all your years with Reece, you are still only an assistant professor?"

"I haven't been with Reece for so many years. I originally joined Reece as an assistant professor seven years ago, but then left after a year. You see, I married—"

"And your husband objected to your working?"

"It's a long story, Mr. Akira." She got into the company car and turned to stare out of the window. "I don't think you'd be interested, really."

He continued as if she hadn't spoken. "But after having left Reece you returned. Didn't your husband object?"

"We were divorced more than eighteen months ago." Certainly, she thought, that would stop the questions, but he only said blandly, "And the circumstances of the divorce?"

"That's none of your business!" she snapped. "My personal life is no concern of yours!"

"On the contrary," he replied calmly, "everything you

do or have done concerns me. We are your sponsors here in Japan, remember? And everything about you reflects on us. How you act, what you say, how you dress . . . you see, Rea Harley, you can give us prestige or discredit us. I believe you Westerners call it 'face.'"

She swung around to face him, her eyes a golden blaze. "Mr. Akira, I'm not asking any favors from you. Your father wants me to do a job for him . . . good. I want help with my book. I'll keep my side of the bargain if you keep yours . . . and then we're quits. But my own life is my own damned business."

For a second, Ivan's green eyes registered surprise, and a triumphant thought flashed through Rea's mind—good, I've told him off! At that moment, she was so angry that she wouldn't have cared if Ivan Akira had stopped the car and asked her to get out. Instead, his mocking smile returned almost instantly, and his eyes became hard. "Just so we completely understand each other," he said, "this is my father's idea, not mine. I'm carrying out his request because it is my duty to obey him. However," he added, and his voice became as cold as his eyes, "I want to make it plain that you will regret it if you cause us to 'lose face' in any way."

He did not touch her, and yet she felt his words almost physically . . . the same way she'd felt the tight grip of his hands that day he'd surprised her in the Wynns' apartment and kissed her so cruelly. She caught her breath, her anger gone as quickly as it had come, and felt herself suddenly alone and somehow bereft.

She forced herself to speak quietly, calmly. "Now that we understand each other, Mr. Akira, I—I think we ought to get on with the day's work. Please tell me a little about Kingo Glass."

For a second, he glanced at her, and Rea thought she saw a touch of admiration in the until-now cold eyes. "The president of Kingo Glass is a Mr. Abbé. He's been to your country, and fancies he speaks English well. Indulge him." A swift smile changed Ivan's face, making it warm, somehow younger. "He's really a very nice man, and will tell you all you want to know about the history of the glass business here in Japan. That should be of interest to you."

Mr. Abbé was graciousness itself. As Ivan had said, he had studied at Cal Tech, and insisted on talking to Rea in fragmented English, which she found hard to follow. "I am too happy to see you," he said several times. "You will have tea? No? Then, later. Now, I am taking you on tour of factory, which is here on premises. You ask questions when interested, please?"

Rea was fascinated by the glass factory. Eventually, Mr. Abbé gave up speaking his stilted English, and they began a long, informative discussion in Japanese. Ivan walked behind them, speaking only when he was asked a question or called upon to translate a difficult concept into either language.

"It is a cheerful factory," Mr. Abbé assured Rea, and she agreed that it was. Just then, she noted a large, life-sized doll made out of inflatable rubber standing in the aisle. Rea was about to ask what the doll was for, when a loud buzzer went off.

"It is only the afternoon lunch break," Mr. Abbé explained. "Most of the workers have their lunch brought into them by firms that specialize in '*bentoh,*' or Japanese lunch." He went on to explain some more, but Rea's attention wandered. She looked around at the relaxed workers and then realized that one of them had not begun to eat. Instead, he had risen from his seat and was walking over to the rubber doll. As Rea watched, he began to pummel the doll with both fists, using it as a punching bag.

She looked at Ivan, but neither he nor Mr. Abbé—nor, in fact, anybody else—was paying him the slightest attention. When the man finally returned to his seat, Rea turned to Mr. Abbé. He laughed.

"The doll is there in case someone is angry or upset about something or at someone. Aggression can be taken out by punching the doll . . . it is better than keeping anger inside," Mr. Abbé explained.

"It certainly is." Rea couldn't help glancing at Ivan as she spoke, and saw a flicker of amusement warm his eyes as he met her gaze. For an instant, she sensed a friendliness in him, an understanding. Then he turned away, and the moment was gone.

The interview lasted another hour, after which Rea and

Ivan thanked Mr. Abbé and took their leave. Ivan said very little until they had reached the office car, and then he turned to her.

"Are you hungry?"

"Thank you, no," she said with dignity. "You were very kind to guide me around the glass factory, but I think your responsibilities for the day are over."

"I'm not talking about responsibilities, but about food," he corrected her. "I'm hungry, and I daresay you must be, too. If you don't want to eat, however, that's fine . . . I'll send you home by taxi. However, I think I heard your stomach growl back there while all the Kingo people were wolfing down their *bentoh*."

Rea was speechless. Worse, her stomach gave another growl, a very large one! Ivan merely said, "Have you ever been to a *sushi* bar?"

"In the States, yes . . . in Japan, no!" She couldn't keep the eagerness out of her tone. "I suppose it is different here?"

"You'll soon find out, professor—I beg your pardon, *assistant* professor!" He leaned forward, directing the chauffeur, then sat back again. As always, Rea was very aware of his physical nearness and the aura of power that he projected even when he sat very still. She glanced at him, saw his fine profile etched against the bright afternoon sunlight. An unwonted thrill filled her as she traced the proud dark head with her eyes, the strong jaw, the powerful nose.

"After all," he was saying, "it would make us lose face if our protégée was found lying by the roadside, fainting from hunger."

It was such a ridiculous idea that she chuckled, suddenly, and then laughed out loud. "I suppose that's true. I warn you, I have quite a disgustingly large appetite." She paused, adding, "It would never do to make you lose face."

She had expected the *sushi* bar to be a splendid place, the kind of restaurant an aristocrat might patronize. Nothing was further from the truth. The chauffeur let them off in front of a tiny shop in the busy Shinsaibashi district, between huge department stores and larger eating houses. Ivan nodded to a blue half-curtain that flapped in the breeze.

"The *sushi* bar," he said.

"In there?"

He paid no attention to the surprise in her voice, but merely parted the curtains to let her pass. Rea walked in and found herself assailed by mouth-watering smells. Rice and fish and egg and vinegar... her stomach growled even louder.

They were in a small room, where customers crowded on stools around a half circle of white polished wood. They called their orders to the chef, who stood behind the half circle and scooped up little balls of white rice out of a wooden tub, topped them with the delicacy ordered by the customer, then slid them out onto the wood.

"What will you eat?" Ivan asked, guiding Rea towards two vacant seats.

His voice was easy, relaxed, and Rea felt none of the tension or hostility of the morning. Instinctively, she realized that Ivan had not accepted her or revised his opinion of her but was offering her a truce.

"Everything looks wonderful," she said. "I warn you again, I love it all. Egg and vegetables and *sashimi*..." His eyebrows rose, and she laughed. "Oh, yes. I adore raw fish!"

Ivan called an order, and *sushi* was slid before them, together with earthenware bowls of green Japanese tea. Rea popped a rice ball into her mouth and chewed, her eyes closed in bliss. When she opened her eyes, another sushi stood before her. Ivan watched her with amusement, but she didn't care. She really *was* hungry.

"When you studied Japanese history and language, you must have also studied its food," he remarked, when she had licked the last grain of her second *sushi* from her fingers. "Not many Westerners take to our food as you do."

"I've always loved everything about Japan. I think I told you I took my B.A. in Far Eastern history? Well, for years and years, it was a dream of mine to come here."

"What happened to the dream?" Ivan asked. Rea frowned a little, but he asked, quite gently, "Your marriage?"

Reluctantly, she nodded. "I suppose so."

He shook his head. "Westerners often protest loudly about romantic love...and are scornful of the Japanese tradition of arranged meetings. Perhaps if you and your husband had had the *omiyai,* you would never have married."

Rea lifted her teacup with both hands, drinking slowly. "I don't know," she said at last. "Perhaps we wouldn't have married, as you say. But . . . some things *have* to be. I think my marriage to Bill was like that."

"You loved him very much," Ivan said. He frowned down at his own empty teacup, put it on the polished wood for a refill. Then, he added, "And now, here you are alone and trying to do everything you wanted to do before your marriage. Like your book."

Rea frowned. She had to make Ivan understand about this book, she thought. She searched for the right words. "The book is something I *need* to do, Mr. Akira. It's a necessity, not a caprice." He was watching her attentively, so she plunged on. "I need to write it, you see. It will help make my position secure at Reece University and get me tenure. Eventually, I will become a full professor there, if I'm lucky."

"And being a professor will make you happy?"

She nodded. "It will mean security," she said quietly. "I don't think you'd understand. You're rich and powerful, and I suppose you've never had to do . . . without. Many days, after my divorce, I had to make a jar of peanut butter and some crackers my whole meal. I'm not crying poverty, you understand, just trying to make you see why I need to write this book. There's a saying in our country: 'Publish or perish.' If I don't get this book done, I'll probably be let go from the staff at Reece, and then it will be back to the peanut butter and crackers."

He seemed genuinely surprised. "I didn't know it was like that," he admitted. "Here in Japan, once you're 'in' as a professor, you're in for life." He drank some more tea and then said, "I can understand your desire . . . for security, Rea Harley."

More *sushi* was ordered, and they ate silently. Rea was glad Ivan had stopped asking her questions. She reflected, ruefully, that he'd probably meant to ask these questions this morning, and had chosen this pleasanter way to "pump" her, but she didn't mind. At least, he finally seemed to understand her position, and it was pleasant in the *sushi* bar. She looked at the people around her, at the *sushi*-maker, who went through the ritual of making new morsels of goodness each time an order was called out. There were grace and design in each created *sushi,* as well as in the simplicity of the surroundings.

"I suppose you want the itinerary for tomorrow," Ivan now said, breaking into her mood. She nodded, realizing that the momentary communication between them had ended, and that it was "business as usual" again. She didn't mind. The more businesslike, the better, she thought as he outlined the next day's schedule for her.

"There's an exhibition of electronic components at Nagoya, so that will be where we go. It's an all-day trip, but I think you'll find it worth your while. The man I will introduce you to in Nagoya built up his business from scratch after the war, and he can tell you a great deal about prewar industry." She nodded quickly. "The day after tomorrow, we're scheduled to visit Kobe. I have some business with some of our textile people there. Then, on the third day, I'm trying to arrange an interview for you with Inada."

Rea looked puzzled. Ivan acted as if the name should be familiar to her. "Inada?" she asked.

"He's quite a powerful figure in Japan . . . controls several of the large TV networks," Ivan explained. "If he's pleased with you, you can take your pick of any talk shows you might want to participate in. Inada's a hard man to get hold of, but he owes us a favor." His calm voice was easy, assured.

Rea merely nodded. She was convinced of one thing. Though Ivan had spoken today about "losing face," she was sure that he had never, ever lost face in his life. She wished now that she had not told him about the bad times, the peanut-butter-and-cracker days. What could such a man know about lacking security? How could a man like Ivan Akira ever understand how it felt to be poor . . . or lonely?

- 6 -

THE NEXT FEW days seemed to prove the truth of Rea's observation. Each new day Rea spent in Ivan Akira's company bewildered her more about his complex, many-faceted personality. One moment, he was concerned, even kind; the next, a haughty aristocrat or steel-eyed businessman. He kept her off balance, always aware of him. Even when he was not near her, Rea felt acutely conscious of his presence. More maddening than this was the realization that he sensed her confusion. However, since their talk in the *sushi* bar, he continued his truce with her, neither mocking her nor outraging her by asking personal questions.

Meanwhile, she accompanied him everywhere. The Nagoya trip was a long, weary one for Rea, but well worth it, for two reasons. First, the man Ivan had come to see was an old gentleman, who received Rea courtously and told her fascinating stories of Japan before the war. They lunched at his home, and as he warmed to his tale, he brought out beautiful artifacts that he had kept from prewar days. Rea touched them reverently, and found herself transported back to those times herself.

The other reason had to do with Ivan himself. In the home of the old gentleman, Rea saw another side of the baron's son emerge. He was courteous, deferential, sensitive, and Rea felt that he was as appreciative of the old man's treasures as she herself was. Later, when the talk turned to architecture, he eagerly joined in, his eyes fresh and eager and his voice full of enthusiasm. At one point, the old gentleman laughed. "Who am I to argue with a student of Nando?" he asked.

Nando? Rea wondered, searching Ivan's face in surprise.

"Do you mean the great calligraphist, sir?" she asked, and the old man laughed and nodded.

"Certainly. Hasn't he told you that he studied under Nando-*sensei?* That great man had a share in the molding of young Akira's character. No wonder he possesses the soul of an artist."

That evening, returning home to Osaka, Rea found Ivan in a quiet, reflective mood. They discussed what the old man had told them about the country and its art as well as its industry, and Rea brought up the subject of Nando.

"I never knew that you had studied with him. Is that why you have that scroll of his?" she asked.

He nodded, a faraway look in his green eyes. "I studied with him as a boy. My mother took me there. She wanted me to learn how to create beauty with my mind and hands..." He paused and turned towards her, his eyes still looking at something from long ago. "It's very strange. Until I was ten, I lived with my mother; I saw her every day of my life. Yet now, I can't remember every detail of her face. I tried to paint her portrait once, when I was in England. It didn't work."

She said slowly, "Isn't that the way with feelings? Sometimes I have a feeling and want to get it into words but can't. I try and try, but I can't express the depths of what I feel."

He was silent, and she glanced at him, half afraid that he would laugh at her. But he was still looking at her, and this time she saw that his gaze was no longer far away, but seeing *her*. Under his steady green eyes, she felt her cheeks grow warm, and she half turned away. Unexpectedly, he reached out to cup her chin in his hand and very gently turn it to face him again. The sea-green gaze held hers, and the touch of his hand against her face started a rippling softness somewhere deep inside her. Only this time, the reaction wasn't just in her body, but within her mind and heart as well.

Her voice quavered a little as she said, "Why are you looking at me like that?"

He did not drop his hand, and his voice was strangely still. "There is something about you that makes me think of her...and yet you're not like her at all. She was tall, and you are not. She was fairer, and she had green eyes, and here"—his fingertip traced her jaw—"she was square, and your face is pointed. Perhaps it is the way your face lit up today when you touched the old works of art. Perhaps it is the way you smile."

His fingers moved up, tracing the line of her mouth gently, almost tenderly. Rea realized she had been holding her breath. There was a tightness in her chest and throat, and it hurt. Then Ivan dropped his hand and turned away, and her breath left her like a sigh. The pain inside her seemed to expand as she glanced towards Ivan. He was sitting only a few inches from her, but he seemed to have withdrawn, removed himself from her completely. She lifted a hand to nervously brush back her honey-brown hair.

"If . . . if I remember, we're to go to Kobe tomorrow?" she asked, breaking the silence. She was relieved when he nodded and spoke in his old crisp way.

"Yes, and you'll find the experience will be different from today's interview. The people you meet tomorrow are after only one thing . . . profit. That's another part of modern Japan, and I imagine you'll need to devote some part of your book to it."

She looked at him in surprise. For the first time since they met, Ivan had said, "your book" without making the two words sound like an insult. As if reading her thoughts, he smiled in his usual mocking manner.

That night, she lay awake thinking of the strange conversation she'd had with Ivan in the car. Alexandra Ivanovna must have been an extraordinary woman, she thought. She had to remind Tucker to let her see her photograph, which he had in his files. She remembered the way Ivan's fingertips had traced her mouth, the way he had looked at her as if to see into her heart. Again, she felt the strange sensation of tightness in her throat and chest, and moved restlessly in her bed. Her body felt hot against the cool sheets, and her face felt hotter still because she could not get the feel of Ivan's hands out of her mind.

The next morning, she felt unsure and edgy as she waited for Ivan to arrive. Dressed in her mauve blouse and the old-standby business suit, she hurried to meet the office car when it arrived. But today, Ivan was different from the man she had seen in Nagoya. Today, he was cool, even curt. They exchanged hardly ten words on the way to Kobe.

The businessmen Rea met in this old port city did nothing to lighten Ivan's mood. She could sense his contempt for these people, and later, when they lunched at the Kobe Port Hotel with a banker, it became very apparent. The banker was a pompous person; he attempted to patronize Ivan, who ruthlessly cut him down to size. Though Rea knew that the man had deserved this treatment, she was upset at Ivan, too.

Later, they drove out to Port Island; from there, Rea could see the bay and watch the many ships anchored in the quiet waters. It was nearly sunset, and the water glittered like silver. "Did you enjoy yourself today?" Ivan asked as they walked away from the car and neared the water.

She glanced at him in a troubled way. "No. I . . . wondered why you were so abrupt with the banker with whom we lunched. That doesn't seem to be your style."

"How do you know what my 'style' is?" he demanded, so harshly that she stared at him, astonished. "You know nothing about me. Don't attempt to pretend understanding, where you are ignorant, professor."

Unsettled by his outburst, she turned back to the sea. "I didn't mean to be rude."

"The man was a boor. He made some insulting remarks about both you and me . . . veiled insults, true, but I will let no one belittle the people around me." He seemed to calm himself with an effort, and his voice became more even. "Well, it isn't important. What's important is tomorrow. You have an appointment with Inada."

"The TV magnate—I remember," she said, and he nodded. "I am really grateful to you," she told him. "For yesterday and . . . and Kobe port, and Inada, too."

"I hope so." His reply was unexpectedly grim. "Inada is one of the sort we met today . . . arrogant, boastful, conceited, without breeding or honor. Unfortunately, he's also powerful and influential, so please try to make a good impression."

"I'll be on my best behavior," she said.

He glanced at her, unsmiling. "I hope so. You have a temper, assistant professor. You want to remember that

Inada can do you a lot of good . . . or not, as the case might be."

"Anything else?" she asked drily.

"Yes. Ask intelligent questions. It might be a good idea if you jotted down tonight the things you mean to ask."

Rea knew that this was good advice, but she resented the tone in which Ivan spoke. "You mean that my questions aren't intelligent?" she demanded.

"I am telling you about Inada," he reminded her curtly. "Also, dress well. Inada is the kind of status-conscious boor who likes to see women dressed like models."

Meaning that she dressed like a frump, Rea thought angrily. For once, the heat in her face was not due to embarrassment. She turned to Ivan. "Do I curtsy on my way out of his office?"

His green eyes glared. "Don't be facetious! All I'm saying is that he's a . . . well, you'll soon find out. Oh, and he's a very busy man, so when he gets up from his desk, that's the signal that the interview is over. Don't hang around asking a lot of questions after he makes it plain the session is at an end."

She calmed herself with an effort. "Thank you," she said, quietly. "I'll try to remember."

"Remember," he then said, "you *are* our protégée, Rea Harley. Whatever you do, good or bad, reflects on us."

As if she could forget, Rea thought, as they drove back towards Osaka. The silence that followed was broken only when they reached the Wynns' apartment, where, Ivan told Rea that he would arrive at nine the next morning to pick her up for her ten-o'clock interview.

"That way, you'll have plenty of time to get there, even with traffic," he said. "We may have to wait awhile in Inada's office, but you won't mind that, will you?"

"Not at all. That way, I'll have time to think up intelligent questions," Rea couldn't resist saying. He gave her a quick look, and then, a surprisingly humorous smile.

"Good night, professor," he said.

Tucker was on his way out the door when Rea arrived. "I'm off to fetch Jan," he explained. "She's an awful driver at night, so when she has night calls, I'm the chauffeur. Have you eaten, or will you wait for us to get back?"

"I'll wait. Anyway, I'm not hungry." She paused. "Tucker, what do you know about Shintaro Inada?"

Tucker's round eyes grew rounder. "'Big Daddy' Inada. Well, not much more than other people know, Rea. He can be as nice as pie or as mean as hell, depending on how he feels at the moment. I've had to be nice to the man, because, in addition to having clout with the TV networks, he has influence with the outfit that controls *Outlook*. Why?"

"I'm meeting him tomorrow," Rea said, and Tucker gave a soundless whistle.

"I'll bet Akira really twisted Inada's arm," he said. "The man doesn't give interviews to just anybody! One thing I'll say for Ivan Akira . . . when the man wants results, he gets them!"

Janet was impressed when she heard about Rea's upcoming interview. "What will you wear, Rea?" she asked. "There's time to shop, you know. Some of the best stores are still open, and you and I can take a run down and find something elegant to pour your lovely figure into."

Rea shook her head. "No," she said. "I'll wear what I've been wearing all along."

Janet frowned. "But honey—"

"But nothing." Remembering Ivan's remarks about her clothes, Rea's mouth formed a stubborn line. Perhaps she *was* the Akiras' protégée, but they didn't own her. And she didn't have the means to run out and buy an expensive dress so that she could impress Inada or anyone else. "I'm going for an interview, not a fashion show," she told the Wynns. "My old suit will have to do."

Next morning, however, she took extra care with her appearance, making sure her navy-blue blouse was clean and fresh looking, accepting Janet's offering of a strand of pearls that went well with the refined French twist into which she plaited her hair. She prayed that Ivan would not make any sarcastic remarks when he arrived, but to her surprise, it was Satoh-san, and not Ivan, who rang the Wynns' doorbell at nine o'clock.

The little department manager was all bows and flustered apologies. Mr. Akira, he said, had been called away on urgent business in Tokyo. "I hope that I will be a good substitute in accompanying you to Inada-san's office," he continued. "It is said that he is a very difficult man."

Rea's heart sank. Somehow, she had counted on Ivan's presence—on having his indomitable, self-possessed strength beside her. Satoh-san was a bundle of nerves. His hand shook so much that when he ushered her out of the Wynns' apartment, he slammed the apartment door on her skirt, tearing a jagged hole in it.

He was so distressed with what he had done that Rea's first thought was to reassure him. It wasn't until later that she suddenly realized what had happened. Here she was, en route to meet the great Inada, and she had nothing to wear! Satoh-san didn't seem aware of her problem.

"Fortunately, it is still early; there is time for you to change," he pointed out.

But . . . change to what? Rea wondered. She couldn't change into a summer dress, or an evening cocktail outfit! All she could do was to mend the tear as best as she could. Luckily, Janet was still home, and perhaps between them something could be done.

There wasn't much that *could* be done. "You've ruined the skirt, kiddo," Janet groaned when their best efforts with needle and thread resulted in a skirt that hung slightly askew and looked mended. "I *told* you we should have shopped last night!"

"Well, it's too late now. I'll have to go as I am and hope I sit most of the time," Rea said. "It'll be all right, Jan; don't worry."

But she knew it was not all right, and Satoh-san's comic dismay when he saw her in the mended skirt proved it. "It is my clumsy fault," he groaned. "I am so heartily ashamed, Harley-san. I wish there were something I could do."

The tear was as obvious as they had feared. When they arrived at Inada's sumptuous office in downtown Osaka, Rea saw the disdain with which the comely receptionist greeted her. The woman was not only handsome, but dressed in a chic outfit that had obviously cost a fortune. She eyed Rea as if she were somebody far beneath her.

"Mr. Inada will see you in a few moments," she said, nodding to some seats near the reception desk. As Rea turned to take a chair, she heard the woman murmur under her breath, "What a *terrible* skirt!"

Rea felt her cheeks flame. Biting her lip, she sat down next to Mr. Satoh and pulled out her notebook, in which she had written several questions she wanted to put to Mr. Inada. They were, she believed, all intelligent questions . . . questions designed to get Big Daddy talking about the history of TV as a media in Japan. She had calmed herself to the point of adding another question to the list, when the receptionist told her that Mr. Inada would see her now.

Rea, trailed by Mr. Satoh, opened a door and stepped into the office beyond. She hoped that she looked confident and calm, but she did not feel either of these things . . . especially since she saw that the great TV magnate was on the phone, his back to the door.

He was, Rea saw, a small, thin man with a fringe of beard, hunched shoulders and large hands with long, predatory fingers. The office seemed to suit him. It was large, decorated with modern furniture, strobe lights and countless TV sets. On the huge desk Inada had set up many photographs of himself with various celebrities. An enormous, larger-than-life photo of Inada himself graced one wall.

His telephone conversation over, Inada swiveled his chair around to survey Rea and Satoh-san. He wore, she noted, tinted glasses that didn't disguise the hostile narrow eyes behind them.

"Yes?" he barked.

Rea bowed. "Good morning. I am Rea Harley—"

"So I heard." He glared at poor Mr. Satoh. "Where is Akira? I heard he was coming today with the . . . professor."

Mr. Satoh launched into a long explanation, but Inada cut him short. "Oh, very well, very well . . . I'm a busy man. Let's get on with this." He pointed to a chair in front of the desk and glanced disdainfully at Rea, taking in her hair, her blouse, her skirt, lingering for a moment on the mended part. "Sit here," he commanded. "Ask your questions, if you want."

He was so rude that Rea found herself torn between fury and laughter. By now used to the courtesy of Japanese people, she found Inada an affront. For a moment, she didn't know how to begin, and Inada pounced. "Don't you know what you want to ask?"

Composing herself, she asked her first question. "In your

opinion," she began, "what influence has television had on the Japanese family?"

He did not answer her directly. "I suppose that question is for your book. Well, I may as well tell you I am not in favor of books written by *gaijin*. Foreigners don't portray Japan as it is."

"All I can say is that I will do my best. I have learned the language and studied the country—"

He interrupted her with a rude sound. "Nevertheless, you are not only a foreigner but a woman. Tell me, how did you become a professor at a university?"

She struggled to remain calm, to take no offense. "I have always wanted to teach. Now, about the question, Mr. Inada?"

He ignored her. "Women need a man to protect them. I am not in favor of women having a so-called career." Abruptly, he rose to his feet. "I am sorry, but this is all the time I have for you. I am a very busy man."

She couldn't believe this was happening. She was being dismissed! She opened her mouth to protest, then stopped. Inada wasn't about to answer any questions or give her any time. He, like his receptionist, had summed her up the moment she entered his office in her torn skirt . . . summed her up and dismissed her!

She got to her feet with as much dignity as she could, and bowed silently. Then, her heart beating fast from humiliation but her head held high, she walked out of the office.

Satoh-san followed her, looking ready to cry. "I'm sorry; I'm so sorry," he moaned.

"It really isn't your fault." In spite of her own misery, Rea felt sorry for him. "Please don't blame yourself."

"It was my clumsiness that began all this. I don't know what I can say in apology to Akira-san. He will be furious." His face was pale. "I won't be able to look him in the eye."

Rea felt a sinking sensation in the pit of her stomach. Now she realized that every word Ivan had said to her had been for her own protection. He hadn't been criticizing her . . . and it was her own fault if she'd taken it that way. "It was *my* doing, Satoh-san," she sighed. "If Mr. Akira is going to be angry with anyone, he'll be angry with me."

And how angry he would be, she thought dismally. How often had he stressed the point that she could be an asset or a liability to the Akiras?

All that day, she listened with dread for the ring of the telephone and Ivan's curt voice telling her how poorly she had done. Neither came. She tried to work, but a sense of complete dejection had come over her, and she found herself crossing out as much as she wrote. Inada's words came back to her: "I am not in favor of books written by foreigners." Perhpas he was right. Perhaps what she was writing was useless tripe. Perhaps Ivan's first reaction to her writing was the correct one after all.

The Wynns' reaction to the Inada interview was to shrug and remark, "Well, you can't win them all." "I wouldn't lose any sleep over it," Tucker told her. "Inada's known for his meanness, as I told you. The fact that Ivan hasn't called to chew you out shows that he knows it too. My advice is to go to bed and write today off."

Before she did go to bed, Rea went shopping with Janet. Though she was appalled at the price of clothes, she knew she couldn't show up the next day in a sundress. She chose a simple beige dress which would do for future business meetings . . . if there *were* any. She was scheduled to go through a soap factory in Itami, near Osaka, and then to interview some of the families of Akira Industries' employees. But would Ivan show up to take her, after today?

Next morning, she tried to act casual at breakfast, show no nervousness. When the doorbell rang at nine-thirty, however, she set down her coffee cup so hard that it slopped over the rim and onto the new beige dress. She ran to sponge it clean while Janet opened the door. Fine impression she'd give, she thought, furious with herself as she dabbed the dress clean and emerged from the bathroom with a large wet spot showing plainly on her bosom. It didn't help that this morning Ivan Akira seemed even more carefully dressed than usual, in a handsome linen suit of light gray. He was talking with the Wynns, but when she came up to him, he turned to her without a trace of expression.

"Good morning," he greeted her, as if nothing had happened. "Ready to go?"

Jan gave Rea a wink, but Rea wasn't fooled for an instant.

Underneath the studied calm on Ivan's face, he was angry or upset. She knew it by the precise way he spoke as they left the Wynns' apartment. "The soap factory should be interesting to you as an example of ingenuity. They manufacture all sorts of things there, you know: soap, fertilizer, candles. Our tour there should take an hour or two, and then I've set up a round-table discussion with our employees' spouses and parents. Is that all right?"

"It sounds fine." Not one word about Inada or the debacle that interview had been! Well, if that was the way he wanted it, she would play his game. Rea glanced at him surreptitiously as they got into the office car, and saw that he had chosen that moment to look at *her*. Their glances caught, and for an instant Rea was conscious of sea-green eyes that seemed to appraise her as completely as Inada's had done.

"You are wearing a new dress this morning," Ivan said, settling himself down in the car seat. She nodded wordlessly. "Beige is a very neutral tone, don't you think? It suits most women."

Was that a compliment? No, a statement. There was nothing complimentary in the way Ivan continued to look at her. Rea felt that she had to bring up the subject of Inada. They couldn't go through the whole day without at least mentioning it!

"About yesterday—" she began.

"Satoh told me about it," he said abruptly.

"It wasn't his fault, no matter what he said. He blamed himself totally, but I think I was to blame."

"I agree."

She turned to face him, her eyes snapping. "I also think that Mr. Inada was the rudest, most unpleasant man I have ever met."

He made a gesture which seemed to mean: well, I warned you. She braced herself for what he might say next, but all he said was, "It is a pity about the torn skirt."

Her defenses crumpled at the new note she detected in his voice. Ivan was not angry, after all. Or if he was, he wasn't angry at *her*. It was ridiculous how relieved she felt, and she forced herself to sound brisk and businesslike.

"I'm sorry I couldn't change. You see, I travel light. A

carry-over from the days with my husband, I suppose, when we traveled around so much. I'm afraid Mr. Inada got a bad impression of American women professors."

"Probably, but that is not your problem." There was a little pause, and then Ivan said crisply, "Forget Inada . . . for now. We have more important things to discuss. Jim Hume has upped his arrival date in Japan. He will be arriving tomorrow evening, and will be here for the Industrial Trade Exposition, which is being held the day after tomorrow." He looked at her thoughtfully. "I had planned for you to visit the exposition anyway, but now you will have to do more than 'just visit.'"

"You mean, you want me to meet Mr. Hume and accompany him around the exposition?"

"More than that. You will accompany him, yes, but you will also be seated next to him that evening at a gala banquet at the Royal. The banquet is for all the businessmen who are exhibiting, so it will be quite a large affair. You will have to entertain Mr. Hume through quite a long evening, I'm afraid."

Rea nodded quickly. "That was our bargain. You've lived up to your end, so I'll do my best for you now."

His steady green eyes surveyed her again, and then he smiled. Again he seemed younger, happier. "That's all we can hope for, Rea."

She caught her breath. It was the first time he had called her by her first name alone, and the sound of it on his lips made her flush with a peculiar pleasure. Then Ivan looked away, the smile vanishing as quickly as it had come.

"As far as Inada is concerned, take it as a lesson. From now on, in any situation, go in to win. Losing gives one a bad taste in the mouth. Let this be the last time you lose at anything!"

His voice was low, but charged with such intensity that she turned to stare at him. He reached out to take her hand and hold it tightly in his own, and she felt as if a surge of electricity had jolted through her. Struggling to gain control of herself, she said, "Why do you say that? Surely you've never lost at anything!"

"I did lose . . . once," he said. "A very long time ago,

I had to stand by and watch a tragedy take place. I was only a child then, and I could not prevent things from happening . . . even though my heart broke and my world was destroyed."

He was still holding her hand, and she felt him tremble. She knew immediately that he was speaking about his mother's leaving Japan. She listened to the sudden raw feeling in his voice and realized that he was telling her something that he had kept hidden within himself for a long, long time. The words came out of him with a steady, aching deliberation.

"My mother and my father both cried that day. My mother said that she could not stay, and my father could not make her stay. I swore to my mother that when I was a man, I would bring her back to Japan, but before I could grow up, she died."

Ivan stopped speaking and drew a long breath that seemed like a sigh. He let go of Rea's hand and leaned back against the car seat. His voice was calm again as he said, "I swore to myself then that that was the last time I would ever be powerless. From that day, I promised myself that I would always be the winner. In everything."

They did not speak again during their ride to Itami, but Rea had plenty to think about. What Ivan had said, explained a great deal about him. But why had he told her all this? She had the feeling that Ivan had never spoken about that time to anyone, not even to his sister. Then why to her? She felt his intensity, the raw emotion in his voice, the grip of his hand, and the same tight feeling she had had on the day of the Nagoya trip flared in her. This time, it was for the little boy who had wept to see his mother and father part. She had been wrong about one thing. Without a doubt, Ivan Akira had known what it was to be lonely.

She still felt subdued when they reached Itami, and the great, noisy, fascinating factory did not completely take away her somber mood. She listened to Ivan talk business and exchange small talk with the factory owner, and wondered how he could so easily change his moods. She herself felt drained. Leter, during the round-table discussion with the Akira Industries employees, she had to strain to keep the discussion going. All the questions she had been so interested in seemed somehow vague and unimportant, and though she smiled and recorded the answers, she could not muster up any great enthusiasm. She was actually glad when the discussion was over.

Ivan seemed to sense this. "Are you tired?" he asked her afterward. "The day seems to have wearied you."

"Does it show?" Rea tried for a light smile, then gave up and shook her head. "I'm sorry. It hasn't been a good day for me."

"Then I will drive you home, and you can get some rest," Ivan said. "You've probably been working too hard."

There was a trace of anxiety in his voice, and Rea felt he was concerned about the industrial exposition. "Don't worry," she said. "I'll be in good shape for Mr. Jim Hume . . . full of questions and encouragement. You'll see."

"I hope so," he said, but his voice had changed again, and when she looked up at him, his face was unreadable. He held the door open for her. "Shall we go?"

To her surprise, he did not use the company chauffeur that afternoon, but drove himself. He explained that the driver had not felt very well and was being given the afternoon off. "It may come as a shock, but I enjoy driving," he told her with one of his quick smiles. "We'll take another route home . . . and you can see some of the sights of Osaka. I don't believe you've seen anything since your arrival except the typewriter and a lot of uninteresting company officials."

"I wouldn't say uninteresting," she said, but she leaned back and looked around her with pleasure as he drove slowly, pointing out various landmarks. He was certainly taking a different route to the Wynns' apartment, but Rea didn't give it any thought till they slowed and stopped in a shopping area unknown to her. "Why are you stopping here?" she asked.

"Business," he told her. "I should say, unfinished business."

"Here?" She looked around at the assembly of shops. Ivan had parked the car in a minute parking space beside a shop called La Charmante, a small, women's boutique.

"Yes, here. My manager tore your dress yesterday, remember? It would cause him to lose face if you didn't accept a replacement. On Akira Industries, of course."

"But I couldn't accept anything like that!" Rea cried. "It's not necessary, Mr. Akira."

"I think it's time you called me by my first name," he said, breaking into her protests. "Madame Inoue, who runs La Charmante, would think it very odd if you continued to address me so formally. She'd probably guess you were a new employee of mine and that I was up to no good, buying you a dress."

He got out of the car, walked over to her side and held the door open for her. "Please, I really don't want a dress," Rea said.

He frowned. "Don't be stubborn. Think a moment. What would you wear to the exposition and to the dinner party afterwards?"

"This . . . and I have my white cocktail dress!"

"All very well and good, but not for the kind of society in which you'll be mingling the day after tomorrow. Come, Rea . . . have you forgotten Inada?"

Rea felt her face flush. "No. But—"

"But if people can't take you as you are, to the devil with them? That might work in America, but we are in Japan. When in Rome . . . you know the saying." Firmly, he held out a hand and took hers, drawing her gently but insistently out of the car. "You are our protégée, Rea. You must make a good impression on Hume." He smiled. "If it'll make you feel better, I will tell you that Akira Industries is putting your bill on the office account as extra expenses."

Still talking, he opened the door of La Charmante. Rea stepped inside the small shop. She was relieved that it was a small store, certainly not extravagant. The clothes, however, did seem to be in good taste. Still wavering, she glanced around her, then at Ivan, who nodded encouragingly. He was right, she thought. She had to make a good impression . . . it was a business expense. Still, she felt odd, as a middle-aged woman in a black dress walked over to them.

"Akira-san . . . how nice to see you," she said, in a cool,

pleasant voice. "Is there something special I can do for you today?"

Ivan explained that Rea was a visitor to Japan, who had two important social functions to attend. "We will leave it in your hands, Madame Inoue," he added.

"Of course." Critically, the woman surveyed Rea, and then nodded. "To go with the eyes, naturally . . . such distinctive eyes." She turned to one of the racks and slid out a dress that was cut simply but with exquisite precision. The color of the dress was a warm amber, but when Madame Inoue moved it, lights danced across the silk surface, and the color changed.

"And this," Madame Inoue added, pulling down another dress. Rea caught her breath. The magnificent creamy silk was so lovely that it reminded her of apple blossoms against an early spring sky.

Madame now motioned Rea to come with her to the one tiny fitting room in the store. "The amber dress first," she suggested.

The garment had seemed simple off, but when it was fitted to her, Rea knew that she had never really owned a *dress* before. This wisp of honey-colored silk fitted itself against her so lightly, so subtly, that it seemed as if it had been made for only her.

"Ah, you are born to wear clothes," Madame Inoue said, sighing in admiration. "With your high bosom and those long, slender legs! I have customers—princesses and the wives of rich, rich businessmen—who would give all their jewels for such a figure." She paused. "Will you show yourself to Akira-san? It would be a crime not to show such beauty." She held open the curtain of the dressing room with an inviting smile.

But Rea shook her head. "I don't think he'd be interested, really. This is just business, you see." Madame lifted her eyebrows, and Rea felt herself flush under those cool eyes. "May I . . . try on the other?"

She forgot her confusion as the yards of creamy silk fell around her. She stared at her face in the mirror. Was this really her? The creature who gazed back at her, lips parted in wonder, was a lithe, golden-eyed beauty with honey-gold hair. From somewhere long ago, she remembered a poem which described a woman as a creature of "silver light and darker gold." This couldn't be her, she thought. She wasn't even pretty.

"Now I insist you show yourself." Madame held open the curtain with determination. "Indeed, you make me want to cry with pleasure, and I am glad to be a designer." She lifted her voice. "Akira-san, don't you agree that the young woman is beautiful in my creation?"

Rea turned from the mirror, her eyes dazzled by what she had seen and couldn't yet believe. Ivan stood outside the dressing room, watching her. To her confused eyes, his expression had changed, had become something like wonderment. Even his voice was different.

"Yes," she heard him say. "You are right, Madame. She is very beautiful."

- 7 -

JANET WYNN'S EYES nearly popped out of her head when she saw the white box from La Charmante. "Oh, Rea, it's *the* store in Osaka. I've heard that Madame Inoue is very selective. She often refuses a customer, no matter how much money she has."

Rea's conscience was troubling her. "I don't know if I should have accepted the dresses. He made it sound so . . . proper, and yet my New England upbringing tells me—"

"That nice girls don't accept dresses from men to whom they are not engaged?" Jan grinned. "I wouldn't give it a thought, dear. As you say, the Akiras consider you their protegée, and they have to have you look super for this exposition and the banquet. And poor Satoh-san will probably feel relieved that his tearing your skirt hasn't ruined your life. When in Rome . . ."

"You sound like Ivan," Rea said, and opened the lid of the box to look down at the soft, creamy-white silk. She remembered the look in his eyes, the astonishment in his voice when he said she was beautiful. "Beautiful," she murmured, stroking the soft material.

"Hum." Janet shot Rea a piercing look, and Rea felt her cheeks grow hot.

"I meant the dress, Jan." Rea said, primly. She closed the box, and yet she could not shut away the memory of Ivan's eyes. Get hold of yourself, girl, she told herself sternly. No more razzle-dazzle . . . remember? Not now. Not ever. Certainly not with a rich aristocrat who hardly knew she was alive.

But that was a lie, and she knew it. This afternoon, Ivan

had been very conscious of her existence. His green eyes had not run over her appraisingly or casually, but had roved from her dazzled eyes and her rapt face to her white shoulders—as creamy as the silk of the evening dress—and to the swell of her high breasts. "Beautiful," he had said, and his eyes had moved over her waist, the curve of her hip. The word had not all been for the dress . . . he had seen her, looked at her as a man looks at a woman he desires. Rea felt a swelling in her breasts, her loins. She turned quickly away from the appraising look in Janet's eyes.

"Now, Rea . . ." Jan began.

Fortunately, Tucker returned home, cutting short any words of warning or caution Janet had seemed ready to speak, and talk at the dinner table concerned the industrial exposition itself.

"Every manufacturer and firm in Osaka will be represented," Tucker told Rea. He explained that the three-day exposition would be held in one of the largest hotels in Osaka. "They have these events quite often," Tucker continued, "but I imagine that Jim Hume's visit has made this exposition a specially important one for the Akiras."

"How will you entertain him, Rea?" Jan questioned. Rea replied that she would concentrate on reading up on Japan's history to refresh her mind.

She spent the next day preparing, but could not really take her mind off the two dresses hanging in the closet . . . and the man who had given them to her.

"No," Rea upbraided herself sharply. She plunged back into the history of feudal Japan . . . only to see, on every page, the handsome, arrogant features of Ivan Akira. He would have made a magnificent lord in those semibarbaric times . . . he would have led men after him in battle, won hearts left and right. "As he probably does right now. Remember Catherina da Silva?" Rea asked herself out loud. "I'm disgusted with you, Rea Harley. *Professor* Rea Harley, damn it!"

The next morning, Tucker whistled when she came to the breakfast table in her tawney silk dress. "Good grief," he said. "If you'd worn that creation to Inada's, he'd have kissed your hand and done whatever you'd wanted."

"Probably," Rea said drily. She hoped Jim Hume would

be as impressed. She wanted to do her best for the Akiras . . . for Ivan. She knew he was counting on her.

She arrived at the exposition early, and was greeted by a smiling, bowing Satoh-san. "I am glad you are early, Rea-san," he said between bows. "Last night, I met Mr. Hume. He is most anxious to meet you and discuss the book you are writing." His little eyes blinked at her aprovingly. "Akira-san praised you very highly, you know." He paused. "Will you come this way? While Akira-san picks up Mr. Hume, I am to introduce you to some of the business people here. There are two industrialists from America whom Akira-san wanted you to meet," he explained.

Rea was introduced to a Carl Johnson and a Philip Epping. Johnson was a florid, rather stout individual with receding hair, and Epping had a sardonic twist to his thin-lipped mouth. Neither of them was overly prepossessing, but Rea was as pleasant as she knew how, because she felt that that was her duty today. Both businessmen seemed cordial enough, and Epping asked how her book was getting along.

"We've heard of you, of course. The foreign business community in Osaka is not that big, and anything out of the ordinary is news," he said. "Your interest in Akira Industries is . . . ah . . . for research only?"

"You're far too attractive to be a businesswoman, anyway," Johnson added.

After a few more remarks, Rea bowed and was led away by Mr. Satoh. Perhaps it was her imagination, but she felt that both men watched her departure with an avid curiosity. She soon forgot this, however, as a party of four men and three women entered the hall. Rea spotted Ivan immediately, and then moved quickly to the serious-faced American man beside him.

"Mr. Hume," Satoh-san hissed. "Oh, he is a very earnest person! I don't believe I saw him smile once since he arrived here!"

Rea's heart sank a little, but she mustered a brave smile and walked briskly over to the newly arrived party. As she did so, she saw that she knew two of the women—Catherina and Midori. Between the two was a small, slender woman in a Japanese kimono.

A look of pleasure filled Ivan's eyes as she approached. He too must be finding Hume difficult to deal with. "There you are," he said. "Please come over here and let me introduce you to some pleasant people." He placed a hand on her shoulder, moving her gently so that she faced the slender woman in the kimono. "Aunt Sachi, may I present Assistant Professor Rea Harley. My aunt, Lady Sachiko."

The little lady bowed deeply, her slender face wreathed in a smile. "Ah," she said. "You are the famous professor my nephew and niece have been talking about."

In Japanese, Rea thanked Ivan's aunt for her family's kindness. The elderly lady's narrow eyes warmed with pleasure. "How well you speak our language. Some day you must visit me in *Matsuyashiki,* Pine Manor. It is the old home of the Akiras, and is in Kyoto. It would perhaps be of some interest to you."

Rea was next introduced to Jim Hume. This thin, nervous scholarly man looked nothing like the businessman Rea had imagined, but she didn't mind. He reminded her of a colleague at Reece, an economic-history enthusiast. Besides, he seemed genuinely interested in her book.

"I have been looking forward to meeting you," he said. "Ivan has been telling me all about your book. Frankly, I admire your courage in starting such a project."

She smiled at him warmly. "Perhaps we could compare notes," she said. "I have been told that you have done a lot of research about historical Japan."

Hume's eyes lit up at once, but before he could speak, one of the other two men stepped forward. He was stocky, short and had a dark mustache across his upper lip. "My turn, Ivan," he demanded. "I haven't met the beautiful professor. either." He faced her and, taking her hand, planted a loud kiss on its back. "I'd imagined you to be one of those glassy-eyed blue stockings, professor! I'm very glad to see that I was completely wrong."

"This is Diego da Silva," Ivan said to Rea. He still smiled, but Rea noticed a trace of reserve in his voice. "You've met my sister, Midori... and Miss da Silva, haven't you? And this is my old friend Hideo Tanaka."

Smoothly, he detached Diego from Rea's side, and together with Hideo Tanaka and the three women moved further into the exposition hall. Left with Hume, Rea braced herself for her task, but it wasn't necessary. Hume was full of questions about her work at Reece, and later about his own interest in the Heian period of Japan.

"Lady Sachiko has graciously invited me down to Pine Manor to see the modern city of Kyoto," he told her. "It seems strange that in the Heian period, Kyoto was called 'the city of peace.' Lady Sachiko says it's anything but peaceful now. It is my favorite time and place in history . . . and I usually bore people the minute I get going on the subject."

He looked at her anxiously, and she nodded reassuringly. Hume wasn't hard to get along with at all. "You can't bore *me,*" she said. "I've loved everything about Japan for as long as I can remember."

"How marvelous!" A blissful look was creeping into Hume's eyes, when his name was called by a businessman advancing towards them. "Will you excuse me?" He groaned. "I suppose I'll have to circulate. Thank goodness we'll have time to talk this evening at the banquet."

Rea watched him go with a feeling of exultation. Her side of the bargain—to entertain Hume—wasn't going to be difficult at all! In fact, she was going to enjoy it! She turned to follow the Akira party, only to come face to face with a small man with tinted glasses and a fringe of beard. To her dismay, she recognized Inada.

Perhaps he wouldn't recognize her! Rea thought. Inada was the last person she wanted to see today. But he did remember her. "Professor Harley?" he asked.

"Good morning, Mr. Inada." She started to pass by him, but out shot one of those long-fingered hands, to grasp her by the wrist. She looked at him in surprise and saw that an ingratiating smile was plastered across Big Daddy's lips.

"Professor, I am glad to see you here today. I most intensely regret that some days ago, I was too busy to speak with you properly." Beads of sweat had gathered on his forehead.

"That's all right," she said in astonishment. "I'm sure you are a busy man, and—"

"Not so busy that I should turn you away like that. Unfortunately, my time is not always my own, and I was nervous about an . . . er . . . important show." He paused.

"I want to know if you'd be interested in a talk show scheduled for the end of this month? It will be a panel discussion featuring some of the most learned professors in Japan. Inariyama from Osaka University will be there."

Rea wasn't astonished—she was stunned! She had heard of Inariyama at Reece. He was an educator with strong progressive and innovative ideas. "I doubt if I'm in a class with Professor Inariyama!" she exclaimed.

His grip on her wrist tightened. "You would be magnificent! I will have an interpreter stand by in case you need any translating done." There was a little pause, and then Big Daddy added, "Please say that you will come!"

"Of course, but—"

"Wonderful!" he crowed. Letting go of her hand, he bowed and backed into the now-crowded hall. "I will telephone you with all the details later. Yes? We are agreed."

"I must be dreaming," Rea muttered. She watched wide-eyed, as Inada slid into the crowd and disappeared from view. Ivan must have spoken to him, she thought, but what could he have said to put fear into Inada? Something had obviously frightened him, for the humble little man of today was nowhere near the dictator of Japanese TV she had met a few days before!

Somewhat dazed, she began to walk across the hall again, intent on joining Ivan's party. As she did so, she heard a voice behind her murmur, "Not a bad-looking broad, Ivan's latest."

"True. Wonder what took him so long to bring her out into the open?"

A snicker made Rea look over her shoulder, and she saw Johnson and Epping, the two Americans Mr. Satoh had introduced to her earlier. They had their backs to her and obviously did not know she could overhear them. Next, Epping commented: "Imagine passing her off as some kind of professor! Professor, my eye. Wonder if she's got to sleep with that dried-up Jim Hume also?"

"Part of her job, I'd expect," Johnson replied, and the two men laughed.

"Don't envy her there, boy. Akira might be exciting, but Jim Hume . . ."

Rea hurried away, her face flushed scarlet and her chest hurting with the anger ballooning in her. Those two creeps, she thought, thinking... thinking that she was some kind of call girl for hire! Dirty-minded and disgusting...

Then she stopped in her tracks and stood where she was, watching Ivan talking to Jim Hume. They were sharing a joke, and laughing together. Was the joke on her?

She was thirty-one—old enough to know that nothing on God's earth came easy, that nothing was free. Yet, she'd sat there and let Ivan Akira manipulate her...

So many things seemed to tie in. Ivan's first impression of her, and his conviction that she'd used her "wiles" to get an interview for her book. His early attitude towards her work. And Inada... who would probably fawn before the powerful mistress of a rich industrialist, while he would dismiss a poor working woman.

"Of course," Rea whispered.

She would be damned. Not for all the free dresses and food and flattery in Japan would she go along with what Ivan Akira had planned.

"I'll leave," she thought. "I'll walk right out of here now, and they can find someone else to fill their bill or do whatever they want." She turned to walk out of the hall, but not before she looked over her shoulder at Ivan.

He was watching her... sea-green eyes seeing her easily, relaxed, as if he were sure of her. At the sight of him, fury rose in her, a humiliation and anger that tore through her like a brush fire.

No, she thought. She wouldn't walk tamely out of that man's life. She'd humiliate him, too. She'd get back at him. Somehow, she'd make him sorry he was doing this to her.

She threw up her head in a gesture of angry pride and began to walk... not toward the door but towards Ivan. He came to meet her.

"I was wondering where you'd gone to," he said lightly. "Jim Hume found you very attractive. He has to leave the exposition soon, and I will go with him, but please stay awhile and chat with my aunt and Midori." He smiled down at her. "Just make sure to leave in time to rest up for the banquet tonight."

She drew a deep breath. "I won't be at the dinner." She hadn't meant to be so blunt, but now that she faced him, she could hardly keep the words pent up.

He frowned. "Don't you feel well?"

"I'm fine. Just say I've had an eye-opener. I've lost my desire to be your Jim Hume's paid companion."

Without another word, he took her by the elbow and marched her outside the hall. Down a carpeted corridor they went, until Ivan drew her into a small adjoining room. "Now," he said, "explain yourself."

"Why should I explain anything?" Anger and humiliation rippled through her in waves as she glared into his suddenly-icy eyes. "I've simply woken up. You don't need me to entertain your Jim Hume."

"Did he say anything to upset or insult you?" Ivan demanded. He grasped her by the shoulders and gave her a little shake. "What's come over you?"

"Your business associates, for one thing," she said drily. "They seemed to understand the situation far better than I did. I'd thought we had one kind of bargain . . . and it seems we have another. I agreed to talk history to Mr. Hume, not be his . . . his . . . not entertain him in other ways."

She watched Ivan's eyes narrow, and then his mouth set in a harsh line she had never seen before. "You think I want you to sleep with Hume?" he demanded.

She nodded, defiant. Half of her willed him to deny it, but he only looked at her wordlessly, his hands still on her shoulders. The warmth of his touch seemed to permeate the silky stuff of her dress, slide into her flesh. She felt his nearness even though she tried to gather her anger around her as a shield.

"You flatter yourself," he said then. His voice held a harsh, deep cynicism. "Don't you know that if sex was what I intended for Hume, I could find a dozen beautiful bar or nightclub hostesses who would be much more exciting than a professor from Reece?"

"Oh!" she cried, too hurt and furious to say more.

"You overestimate your sex appeal, professor," he mocked her. "You haven't learned anything, have you? Well, I wouldn't want you to go away mad . . . or disappointed."

His hands tightened on her, pulled her close to him. "Stop it," she gasped, but his fingers were like steel . . . molten steel that moved from her shoulders down to her arms, pulling her closer and yet still closer, as if he wanted to pull her inside him. She felt the powerful ripple of muscles against her breasts as he bent to kiss her. His lips were arrogant and demanding, punishing her mouth, ravaging it as he ruthlessly explored it. The scent of him was everywhere, the smell of his after-shave, and the strong maleness that was uniquely his. Rea felt dizzy in his arms, and her mind reeled still more as she felt her breasts being caressed, explored, exploited . . .

Blood thundered through her like the beat of primitive music. If he didn't stop kissing her, she would faint. No, not faint . . . she would not faint. Her body felt warm and sensuous and swollen, ready for love, ready for his hands and mouth and his aching maleness. She couldn't think any more, beyond the feel of being in his arms. A low, passionate moan ripped from her throat.

Then, as brutally as he had dragged her into his arms, he thrust her away. She stared up at him with dazed, half-blinded eyes.

"You will come to the banquet tonight," he said. He was breathing hard, but his voice was deadly cold. "You will come looking your loveliest, in that dress that is like milky-white cherry blossoms. You will not disgrace our company."

She shook her head mutely and raised her shaking hands to her bruised mouth. He went on, inexorably, "You are going to be Hume's learned and most-charming dinner companion. Do you understand? We have a bargain, you and I. I have fulfilled my part. Now it's up to you to do your share." He stopped talking and began to walk away from her, pausing at the threshold of the little room to look back at her. "Once you do that, you are free. I don't care if I never see you again."

- 8 -

REA RETURNED TO the Wynns' apartment from the exposition feeling drained. Mentally and physically tired, she dragged herself to her bedroom and stripped off the tawny gold dress. Gently, she folded it in its box and replaced the cover. She would never wear it again, she thought, never after today. She saw herself, in a flashback, returning to the exposition with Ivan . . . saying goodbye to Hume, even chatting with Midori and the gracious Lady Sachiko. If she was lucky, no one had known what agony each word cost her, and Ivan would never know. . . . But she had to admit it to herself—she wanted Ivan Akira . . . wanted him shamelessly, shamefully.

After all, she wasn't a kid. She'd heard about women newly divorced and crazy for men . . . had pitied them their fruitless, insatiable craving. She herself had wanted no part of men after her divorce from Bill, had only halfheartedly dated one or two people during her eighteen months of being single. So why now, why Ivan Akira? Knowing she'd never be able to sleep before tonight's dinner, she went into the kitchen, where she found Janet mixing drinks.

"How did it go?" Janet asked.

"Good," Rea said. "But then, there's still this evening. After that, the Akiras and I are quits."

Jan gave her a strange, knowing glance. "Oh? I see."

"And what do you see?" Rea demanded. She felt edgy and unhappy and ready to quarrel.

Janet said calmly, "I see that something's happened to make you look all upset and nervous. Want a drink?" Rea shook her head. "Then take some advice from an old lady.

Ivan Akira is as sexy as God ever made a man, but he's not the kind of guy for you. I'm not even sure he's the kind of guy for any woman."

Rea said nothing. Was her desire written all over her face? she wondered. Jan continued, "You had it hard with Bill, Rea. You need peace and serenity . . . a time to heal and come to terms with yourself. That's what you came here for, remember?" She held up a hand as Rea began to speak. "Oh, I know . . . you came to write your book. But deep down, you also came here to get your head together. You are not going to do that with Ivan Akira in your life."

Rea sat down in a kitchen chair and leaned her cheek against her arm. "Am I that transparent?" she asked, and then laughed, a little ruefully. "Of course, you're right. And Ivan isn't in my life, Jan. After tonight, he'll be out of it."

Janet insisted that Rea lie down and rest before the evening, but rest was something Rea didn't dare do. If she lay down, the memories would come again . . . memories and feelings and treacherous sensations. Instead, she helped Jan dust and tidy the little apartment, pausing now and again before the long, white-and-black tranquility of Nando's calligraphy. Somehow, the sight of it rested her, calmed her. By the time she had to dress for the banquet, she was in control of her emotions.

Dressing was a bittersweet experience. Rea knew she looked beautiful in the creamy silk dress, but she remembered the feeling she'd had when she first tried it on. She'd been dazzled then, she thought sadly. It was time to grow up. It was just a pretty dress. And to Ivan Akira, it was only a business investment, and probably one he was regretting at the moment just as much as she was.

In the living room, Janet and Tucker made appropriate comments about her appearance. They looked so comfortable together, Janet with her cap of gray curls disheveled because she'd pushed her reading glasses up on top of her head, Tucker in his slippers run down at the heels, that Rea felt a pang of physical pain. They're happy, she thought . . . happy and together. They belong to one another. The thought stole into her mind that she did not belong to anyone, and she sternly put it away. "I wish both of you were coming."

"Me, too," Tucker said, "but journalists are personae non grata at this big gala. You'll tell us all about it tomorrow. I imagine you'll be coming in quite late."

Not if she could help it, Rea thought later as she rode the escalator up to the second floor of the Royal Hotel. A bowing maître d' escorted her to a large banquet room. It was brightly lit, and a long, official-looking table at the far end of the room was flanked by a few smaller tables. Several guests had already arrived and were sitting at the tables. As Rea entered, Diego da Silva came up to her.

"How nice you look, Rea," he said, taking her hand and kissing it, as he had done that morning. "Come, I will take you to our table. We are all sitting together . . . more pleasant, is it not? My daughter, Catherina is here, and Midori, and the young man Hideo Tanaka. Ivan and Mr. Hume will join us very soon."

"Is Lady Sachiko not here?" Rea asked as she took his arm and allowed herself to be led into the enormous room.

"Oh, no. Her ladyship is old-fashioned Japanese . . . she allows her men to entertain outside of the house and does not mix in business affairs." He smoothed his mustache sentimentally. "My dear late wife was of the same mind. I was forced, like most businessmen in Japan, to take my clients and associates to nightclubs. My daughter, however, is very modern. . . ."

The table was covered with a snowy cloth, decorated with a basket of fresh flowers, and the silver gleamed beside fine crystal. The diamonds glistened in Catherina's ears as she nodded to Rea.

"How very nice that you could come," she drawled, playing the part of the hostess quite naturally. "Ivan and Mr. Hume have not yet arrived. Midori and I have been talking about their lateness."

Rea smiled at Midori, but the young woman's answering smile lacked its usual vivacity. She was clearly displeased about something, Rea thought. However, Ivan's sister said, "You look lovely tonight, Rea."

"A new dress for the occasion," Catherina said with a graciousness that was almost condescencion. "Did you bring it with you from the States?"

Before Rea could reply, she saw Ivan and Jim Hume walking towards their table. Ivan towered over the slender businessman, and it seemed to Rea as if heads turned as he passed. And well they might, she thought wryly. He looked elegant in a white dinner jacket, the immaculate jacket and linen showing off his warm olive skin.

She turned her attention to Jim Hume, who brightened when he saw Rea, and drew his chair as close as possible to hers. Then, almost immediately, he plunged into the conversation that had been interrupted that morning. As they discussed the Heian period, Rea noted that the two businessmen she had met that morning had come in and were seated at a table some distance away. They were probably thinking that Jim Hume's eagerness was caused by some indecent proposition he was making to her, she thought. Well . . . let them think what they wished. She caught Ivan's glance, and he flashed a small sardonic smile.

She paid no attention to him, or to anyone but Jim. His conversation enthralled her, and it was only when the meal was over and the long, dull speeches began that she was conscious of her table companions—Catherina, with her hand resting lightly in the crook of Ivan's arm, Hideo looking unhappy, Midori mutinous. What *was* wrong with Midori? Rea wondered. It was completely unlike the pert young woman to sulk.

Between speeches, Jim again caught her attention. "Something just hit me. Ivan has arranged for me to go and meet Nando tomorrow . . . the great calligrapher. I would like you to come with us."

Rea hesitated. She was torn between the genuine desire to meet the master and her disinclination to see Ivan again. "It would be useful for the book you are writing, I know," Jim Hume went on. "You know, talking with you has been inspiring . . . and enlightening! I have decided to start on my own book as soon as I get back to America."

"How wonderful," Rea said with real pleasure. She had taken a liking to the intense businessman. "And . . . yes, I would like to see Nando with you. Are you sure it will be all right with Mr. Akira?"

"Of course! Ivan himself suggested I invite you." He

turned to speak with Ivan, and Rea focused her attention on Midori.

"Are you having a good time?" she asked the young woman.

Midori came close to snorting. "A good time? Well, no, I am not. You wouldn't be having a good time, either, if you were on some *omiyai* fixed up by your family!"

An arranged date! Rea stared hard at Midori. She remembered Ivan's mentioning the *omiyai* some days ago. "But these days, doesn't an *omiyai* mean very little?" she asked gently. "You can always refuse to go out with the young man again."

"Much you know," Midori pouted, and continued in a low voice, "Hideo is a dear friend of my brother's, and his father is a dear friend of my father's. Do you understand? They *want* to get us together. And I can't stand him!"

Rea glanced at Hideo Tanaka, who was talking to Diego da Silva and Catherina. He was small and slender, and wore glasses, which seemed to slide down his nose every other moment.

Just then, however, Jim Hume started to speak with her again. She was rapt by his knowledge of Japan, and was surprised to see out of the corner of her eye that Midori had risen and was stalking away from the table.

"That sister of mine," Ivan muttered. "Now, what . . . ?"

Rea turned and saw Catherina following Midori, obviously talking to her. Diego and Hume were bending across the table, talking to Hideo, who had started out of his chair.

"I'd better go see what's wrong," Ivan said grimly.

He stood up from the table and paused. Rea heard Diego saying, "It's just a game with Midori. I'm sure she didn't mean any of the things she said."

"What happened?" Rea asked.

"Midori said she didn't want to sit through the rest of the evening with Hideo," Diego said. "She said she was going home . . . by taxi, if necessary," he added. He looked a little nonplussed. Apparently, well-bred Japanese ladies did *not* do this sort of thing. "Catherina's talking to her."

"I'll go see what's happening," Ivan said. He turned to Hume apologetically. "I'm sorry about this, Jim."

"Nonsense. Rea and I will pick up where we left off,"

Jim Hume said. He looked at her as he spoke, and Rea nodded and tried to smile, but her eyes were on Ivan's tall figure as he walked away. She had the irrelevant impression that as he went, he took all the light and brightness of the room with him . . . and, she had the very clear knowledge that no matter what she knew to be right for her, there was no way she could cut Ivan Akira out of her life.

- 9 -

RISING LATE THE next day, Rea hurried to pack her camera and tape deck in her shoulder bag. She had promised to meet Jim Hume and Ivan at Akira Industries. Congestion around Mido-suji made her late by about five minutes, and when she reached the Akira Industries building, she ran up the stairs and through the sliding glass doors.

Ivan was in the foyer, waiting for her. She looked around quickly, but there was no sign of Hume. "Where is Jim?" She asked, surprised. "Is he late also?"

"No. He had to catch an earlier flight out than he'd expected, because of some business developments back home." She realized what he was saying, and her heart fell. He seemed to read her mind. "However, that doesn't mean you can't meet Nando-sensei. The great teacher is awaiting us, after all."

"But you are so busy! The exposition . . ."

"Satoh and the others can take care of the exposition. That is, unless you don't want to see Nando."

His eyebrows had risen over those clear green eyes, and Rea felt a tinge of the old mockery in his manner. "Of course I want to meet him." She squared her shoulders firmly. "It would be very kind of you to take me to him."

He gestured towards the door. "I've decided to take my own car rather than the office car," he said. "The chauffeur is busy running Satoh back and forth from the exposition anyway, and we will probably be gone a few hours." He led her towards the back of the building, to the parking lot there. Like all parking lots in Japan, this one was small and crammed with cars, but Rea saw the creamy white Lancia right away.

"That has to be your car," she exclaimed.

He laughed. "Is it that obvious? An extravagance, but I bought it while in the States, and brought it back with me." He held open the door of the sports car. "After seeing it, no other car would satisfy me."

She felt the luxurious softness of the car seats, and nodded when Ivan asked her if she preferred to drive with the top down. "I like to feel the wind in my hair," she confessed. "My father had a very old convertible when I was growing up. We used to take Sunday drives, and there was always a battle between my mother and us. Mom hated to feel so much as a puff of air. Dad and I loved to drive with the top down."

He got in beside her and started the car, backing it smoothly out of the parking lot. "Your parents live in Boston?"

"No . . . they're dead now." There was a small silence between them while Rea had a fleeting memory of their small family rambling down a New England road with the green leaves of early summer catching the light of the sun.

"I spoke with my father this morning," Ivan said, breaking the silence. "He was very pleased with your success with Hume. You certainly accomplished all that we hoped for."

"He was an interesting man," Rea said. "Not at all—"

"—the kind of man you expected him to be?" Ivan finished the sentence for her. Rea's cheeks warmed at the memory of Johnson and Epping's remarks, and she cast around for a safer topic.

"How is Midori?" she asked.

Ivan shook his head. "I can't understand her. She made a scene at the one time when I wanted her to act like a proper lady."

"Perhaps it was not the time for an *omiyai,*" Rea pointed out. Ivan frowned, but nodded after a moment.

"You are right. It was poor timing. Yet, Hideo was going to the exposition and the banquet anyway . . . and he had wanted to go out with my sister for such a long time. In any case, her behavior last night was disgraceful."

"Perhaps not disgraceful," Rea said gently. "She's very young."

He glanced at her, amused. "Does that mean you don't approve of the custom of arranged dating? It must be fascinating to a social historian. But Japanese women are different from women in your country."

"Indeed?" Rea asked, then leaned back, eyes crinkled against the sunlight as the Lancia picked up speed.

"Of course. One of the differences is that a Japanese woman wouldn't show all her feelings in her face or actions . . . as you so often do." She opened her eyes to find him smiling at her. "As you are doing now."

"But . . . why not?" she argued. "What is there to hide? Is it better to conceal emotion, hide behind a—a mask? A mask of mockery, perhaps, or laughter?"

He was suddenly serious. "You yourself have many masks, Rea. You should know that they serve many purposes." He paused, then added casually, "While talking to my father this morning, he told me that he is considering another line of goods."

"Expansion?" she asked. He nodded, and she studied his profile. Etched against the early-afternoon sun, he seemed chiseled from gold. No, not gold . . . that was too hard, too unmalleable. The material from which Ivan had been sculpted was fluid, graceful, and yet tougher than any metal. Like moonlight on water, she thought . . . beautiful and unreachable.

"My father is always interested in expansion. His dream is to build an enormous business empire stretching across the sea. In the ancient days, members of my family were *Daimyo* . . . lords of wealth and power. My father wants us to control the business world as the old lords did." There was a pause, while Rea thought of Ivan in breastplate and helmet, and then he said, "He is also considering a merger between Da Silva Techmatics and our company."

"Diego da Silva's company."

Ivan nodded. "They have been negotiating for months, but I believe they are close to an agreement. Both Diego and my father are hard-headed businessmen."

They then enjoyed a comfortable silence as Ivan drove

out of Osaka proper and down the Meishin highway towards Kobe. "Are we very far from Nando-sendei's house?" Rea asked some time later, as Ivan turned off the Meishin and drove down a narrow one-way street. A few bicyclists, women with shopping baskets on the backs of the bicycles and wearing large hats against the sun, rode leisurely by. "Are we in Kobe?"

"No . . . we are in Ashiya. Nando-sensei makes his home near the Ashiya river. He told me once he moved here because in the spring the cherry trees are magnificent around the Ashiya-gawa."

Rea now saw fine old homes, bordered by the traditional high gates. After a while, Ivan turned into a street just broad enough to admit the Lancia. When it broadened so that two cars could just about pass each other without touching, he stopped. "We are here."

Rea pushed back her windswept hair and looked about her. Down the street, some distance away, a small river raced under a curved stone bridge. Across the bridge was an "old" Japanese house. "That is where Nando-sensei lives," Ivan said.

They got out of the car, and though Rea looked at it doubtfully, Ivan assured her the bridge would be safe. She followed him over it, and stood beside him as he knocked on the wooden door in the gate. A short time passed, and then an elderly woman's voice asked, "Who is there?"

"It is Jun Akira," Ivan said courteously. Instantly, the wooden door swung open, and an old lady, silver-haired, her back bent, was bowing to them. She was dressed in a gray summer kimono, and as she bowed deeply, work-worn hands rested on her knees. Ivan and Rea both bowed back, and Rea saw that Ivan bent his head with the greatest respect . . . much lower than she had ever expected that proud dark head to bend!

"This is Rea Harley, the professor from America," Ivan went on, and now the old lady bowed to Rea, who murmured her gratitude at being allowed to pay her respects to Nando-sensei.

"The teacher is in his studio," the old lady said when the ritual bowing was over. "Please come this way."

The house was very small, and so, Rea discovered on

reaching it, was the artist's studio. It was a five-tatami-mat room, with one beautiful scroll and a flower arrangement on the *tokonoma,* and a large low table on which an elderly man was working. A sheet of white paper was before him, and his brushes and inks. When he saw them come in, however, Nando looked up with pleasure.

"You are welcome," he said, smiling. "Welcome, Jun Akira, and welcome to you, American professor." His face was round and rosy, and the skin was fresh and free of wrinkles in spite of his white hair.

"Good afternoon, *sensei,*" Ivan said, giving Nando the title of respect. "I have been away from here too long."

"It is so." Nando pointed to the work in front of him. "See what poor work I am engaged in at the moment."

Rea didn't think it "poor work" at all—priceless was more like it. Jan had told her that as he was designated an "Intangible Cultural Property," Nando commanded very high prices for his work. The square of white paper with the bold calligraphy racing across it was the work of a genius—even her unpracticed eyes could tell that.

"A haiku by Buson," Nando said. "Can you read it, Rea-san?" She came nearer and knelt beside him, trying to make out the flowing characters.

"I am not learned, *sensei,*" she said. "I think it has something to do with rain . . . and evening."

"Very good!" He beamed, then read, "'The evenings of the ancients were like mine, this evening of cold rain.' Do you understand what this means?"

"Yes," she said. She could picture Buson sitting in a small Japanese house like this one and listening to the cold rain on the eaves. She could feel his yearning to understand his people, the history of his country. "I've often felt," she said thoughtfully, "that when I studied history, the people—the old people—were even more real than myself."

"Ah, you do understand." Nando appeared satisfied. He nodded as his wife appeared with a tray of tea and small cakes. "You have a Japanese heart, American professor, do you know that?"

She was deeply pleased at the compliment, but as she took the fragile porcelain cup from Mrs. Nando, she knew it was more than that. Nando-*sensei* had said what he perceived to be the truth. The tranquil eyes were now studying Ivan.

"You do not practice the art now, Jun Akira?"

Ivan shook his head. "I regret, no," he said. "There seems very little time."

"Ah, you are busy being a good son to your father." The old man nodded gently. "Yet, there is the *giri*—duty—to your mother, also. Your hands were made to shape beautiful things as well as to sign business contracts."

The talk became more general then, moving to calligraphy as an art both in ancient Japan and in modern times. Rea took notes and many photographs. "I don't believe that the photos will do justice to your work, however," she said to the old master regretfully. Not photographs, not a tape recorder, not even memory, would bring out fully the beauty and tranquility she felt sitting in the simple little studio near this old man with the serene eyes.

He laughed gently. "A photograph is only a part of the picture, Rea-san. It shows only as little as a sparrow's tears. Meditate. Think about what you wish to convey in your work. Make your work a part of your soul."

He took the white square of paper before him and held it out to Rea. "Take this with you, to remind you of an old man," he said gently.

She blinked at him, totally amazed. "*Sensei,* I can't accept—"

"And why not?" He took her hand and laid the paper with the lovely words in it. "Buson wrote the poem, and you understand it in your heart. It is yours." He smiled at them both. "Come again and see me before too long," he added. "I have greatly enjoyed your coming."

Rea hardly felt the tatami under her feet as they left the house. "I feel as if . . . as if I've visited with royalty," she said when she and Ivan were outside the gate.

"Nando is better than royalty," Ivan agreed somberly. His eyebrows were pulled together, and he appeared deep in thought. "I've never seen him give anyone a piece of his work before."

"You don't think I should have accepted it?"

Ivan did not reply. They stood in the narrow road, the hot June sun beating down on them. Above them, from

Nando's cloistered garden, came a rustle of bamboo, the sound of a bird singing.

"Are you hungry?" Ivan asked abruptly. "I forgot about food in there, but now . . ." He gave her a rueful smile. "Tea and cakes don't fill anyone up, and you, I remember, have a large appetite."

She had to laugh. "Is there a *sushi* bar nearby?"

"Better than that. There's an old-fashioned teahouse within walking distance. The food is good, and we can have a private room with a view of a Japanese garden. It's called the Chrysanthemum. We'll leave the car where it is. No one will bother it."

They soon reached a building shaped like a sprawling Japanese house. Rectangles of blue cloth adorned with white chrysanthemums streamed from the wooden door. Ivan pushed the curtain aside and called a greeting, which elicited a hearty *"Irashiai-mase!"* from within. Almost immediately, a plump little maid had them divested of footgear and walking towards a small, interior room which looked out into a Japanese garden. A tiny waterfall surrounded by tall green Japanese pampas was the garden's main feature.

"Do you approve?" Ivan asked Rea.

She nodded, firmly. "I most certainly do. I am glad you brought me here, Ivan."

There was a strange look in his eyes. "Then I am glad too," he said.

The maid brought sitting cushions and tea, and then took Ivan's order for lunch. She soon brought in the meal . . . soybean soup, grilled fish and vegetables carefully arranged in tiny porcelain dishes. Rea and Ivan ate, enjoying the good food and plain white rice, and only when they had finished did Rea lean back with a sign of pleasure. Ivan looked up at her swiftly, a smile in his eyes.

"You've eaten enough?"

"I have gorged myself to the point of pain." She felt comfortable and happy; some of the tranquility she had felt in Nando-sensei's studio must have stayed with her. "It will require an effort to get back to work."

"Let the work rest for a moment," he said.

Something in his tone made her look up at him quickly. He was still watching her with a smile, but there was a tension about him, a sudden intensity, that put her on her guard.

"You work too hard, Rea," he continued. "To paraphrase Nando-*sensei,* a woman should do more in life than write books and teach. You should find someone who will give you time to enjoy the beautiful things that make you smile with your golden eyes."

Her heart had started to hammer. Carefully, she pushed aside her teacup and reached for her purse. "I suppose I just haven't found someone," she said lightly.

"Haven't you?"

She turned quickly, and at the same moment he pushed the low table aside and reached for her. She did not move fast enough to avoid the outstretched hands that drew her closer. . . . She did not want to avoid them.

"You knew when you came here with me today," he said quietly. "Didn't you?"

His arms were around her. She felt herself half water, half fire, her bones weak and melting, and every vein, every cell of her body alive with desire. Yes, she had known. She had known probably from the first time they had looked at each other across the crowded Royal Hotel reception room . . . and he had smiled at her as if seeing her alone.

He tipped back her head, and instead of kissing her mouth, pressed his lips in the hollow of her throat. *"Duschenka,"* he murmured. "Dear little one . . ."

A fire was raging through her, flames of a desire as wild and as ungovernable as a storm. A fierce sob escaped her lips as he drew her to him. He slid down the zipper of her dress, then pulled down the barrier of cloth over her lace-covered breasts. His lips moved from her throat, pushed away the lacy brassiere, roved across her breasts. She moaned as she felt the tender fullness of her nipples being teased and tormented by his mouth.

She cradled his face in her hands, feeling the taut leanness of his jaw, the hollows of his temples near the sweep of his dark hair. My love, she thought, my love . . .

He drew her across his knees so that she was reclining in his arms. Leaving her breasts, his mouth found hers, lips warm with a heady, sweet desire that was so unlike his previous rough kisses. The muscles of his shoulders and arms cradled her and protected her, lying against his powerful body.

"Rea," he whispered against her mouth. He had unbuttoned his shirt, and she felt against her hands and breasts the warm, sweet texture of his skin. I should stop this now, Rea thought, I should stop . . . and yet, she could not stop. She felt herself sinking into his embrace, into *him*, into this poem of love and desire. The sound of the small waterfall outside merged with her breathing, her heartbeat. When Ivan lowered her gently to the golden-matted floor, she drew him down to her with a low sob of joy.

Rea lazily drifted down from heights of rapture so intense, she could hardly bear them. She felt satisfied, her body drugged with joy. Yet, all her senses were keenly aware—of the sounds of the waterfall outside, the tatami mats beneath her, and most of all, of Ivan beside her. She moved closer to him, to the solid, powerful, sensitive body that had given and taken so much pleasure.

"Duschenka," he again whispered. He held her closer, and she sighed, thinking that in Ivan's arms, there was an end to all longing, all loneliness. "I've always wanted you, Rea," Ivan was saying, softly. "I knew I wanted you the day we met. Remember how I telephoned you after the party at the Kin-Bara? I wanted to see you again. You stirred me as no other woman has. . . ."

His hands were moving again, stroking her back, sending ripples of desire through her. Rea could sense the renewal of his wanting her, and every nerve of her body, every fiber and every cell, ached for his kiss, his touch, the sweet weight of him. And yet, the word she herself had conjured in her mind stayed with her, nibbling at her happiness.

Loneliness. Her mind slid back from the pleasure of the moment to the long, lonely hours she'd spent waiting for Bill . . . the bleak nights alone when she had bitterly regretted her lost career, the lost years, the children she had never had. She tried desperately to push those memories away and concentrate on Ivan and the moment, but the memories pressed close.

She had loved Bill . . . and she had let him use her in his heedless, unthinking way. She recalled how he had left her, and that memory fused with more recent remembrances. The snickers of Johnson and Epping . . . Ivan's talk about the merging of Da Silva Techmatics and Akira Industries . . . Babette's insinuations that she was sleeping with Ivan. What future was there for her and this man? None. They were worlds and cultures apart. He would use her for his pleasure and then go on . . . leaving her, as Bill had done.

Suddenly, she was afraid. Afraid of what she was feeling for Ivan, afraid of the future. She struggled to push herself erect in his arms, but he laughed softly and drew her to him, kissing her, bringing her back into that whirlpool of desire. Her entire body was throbbing with wanting him. Desperately, Rea formulated one thought out loud.

"Ivan, what happens after we make love?"

"Whatever you like. I'm not expected back at the office, and the maids here are very discreet. We won't be disturbed."

He had planned this . . . had assumed that this would happen and that she would go readily into his arms. Rea shook her head, as if to clear it. "Ivan, we . . . we can't. We can't do this again."

His tone was one of amusement. "Rea, you sound like a child. We are both adults, and we want each other. Is there anything wrong with that? You're a beautiful woman." Sensually, almost lazily, he began to kiss her throat, her shoulder, her breasts.

With an effort that was like wrenching away a part of herself, Rea pulled herself loose from his arms. "You promised me once that you'd never lie to me, Ivan." He nodded, a small frown between his eyebrows. "Can you tell me whether there's a point in our—in our meeting this way again? You have your life. I have mine. I'm not like you, Ivan. I couldn't just have a casual affair and—and then go on with my life as if nothing had happened."

He said, "But you wanted this to happen, Rea. Be honest with yourself. You wanted me to make love to you."

Rea was silent. How could she explain to Ivan what she only dimly understood herself? How could she make him understand that if she loved him again, she might be lost forever? How to make him see that if he took her back into his arms, she might leave career and homeland for his sake?

She said hesitantly, "I came to Japan to write a book—"

"Your book!" The warmth had left his face, and his eyes were green and hard. "It's always your work for you, isn't it? You can't forget those things long enough to admit you're a normal woman with a woman's needs and wants."

Rea turned away from him and, fumbling, began to put on her discarded clothing. "I can't see you again," she said. The words cost her so much to say that when he nodded easily, she felt herself betrayed.

"As you wish," he said, and she felt something shatter within her. What had she expected he would do? Beg her to see him again? That wasn't the way Ivan Akira was made. She wondered if he'd really felt anything for her besides a casual desire. Certainly, his face was cool and indifferent as he began to dress.

She forced herself to speak calmly, casually. "It must be late . . . time for both of us to get back to work. I—I imagine that we need not meet again."

- 10 -

FOR THE REST of that week, Rea kept that vow. She pushed Ivan Akira into a corner of her mind and resolutely refused to think or talk about him. Her work was important now.

But when Jan called her to the phone one afternoon, saying that there was a call from Akira Industries, Rea's treacherous heart leaped with a wild surge of hope. With deliberate slowness, she went into the kitchen and took the receiver from Janet. "Rea Harley here," she began.

"Rea-san?" Rea's heartbeat slowed with a painful swiftness as she heard Satoh-san's voice on the other end. "You haven't forgotten that Inada has you scheduled to appear on television on the twenty-sixth? He telephoned me here today. He's very anxious for you to come to the studio before that date, to make sure you understand what's going to happen."

Rea *had* forgotton. She glanced at the calendar Jan kept above the phone. The twenty-sixth was only a few days away. "He said he'd be in touch with me, and when he didn't do so, I thought . . ." She bit her lip. She'd thought Inada had dropped her when he learned she and Ivan Akira weren't a pair after all.

Mr. Satoh suggested that he take Rea to the studio the following day. "As you know, there will be many professors on the panel discussion. You need to make a good impression," he said.

"That's very kind of you, Satoh-san, but I can go myself." He expressed horror. It was unthinkable that she go alone. Akira-san had strickly ordered him to take her. Could she be ready tomorrow morning at about ten?

Rea felt tense as she hung up the phone receiver. Ivan

still concerned himself with her. Was it possible he would be with Satoh-san when he accompanied her? The thought made her cheeks grow painfully hot, and she vividly recalled their last meeting . . . the cool tatami mats on which they sat, the rasp of his silk shirt against her breasts, his lips, warm and passionate on hers.

The next day, however, it wasn't Ivan, but Satoh-san, who arrived to take her to the large TV studio and who stood beaming at her while Inada treated her like a V.I.P. Satoh-san also arranged to fetch her in the office car on the twenty-sixth.

"I will be there to see how well you appear on the television," he said with an almost paternal air.

Rea spent a lot of time preparing for the panel discussion. She read several translated works by the professors who would appear with her, notably the essays of Inariyama. By the twenty-sixth, she was ready and eager to debate many of their ideas. When she was driven to the studio and introduced to her fellow panelists, they were pleased and surprised at her knowledge.

The discussion itself was lively. Several of the professors on the panel were for Japanese education as it stood; Inariyama and the only Japanese woman on the panel spoke out for change. Rea found herself speaking freely in Japanese, only rarely being stumped by a hard word in Japanese educationalese. When the show was over, Professor Inariyama invited her to a lecture at Osaka University the following week. Satoh-san was impressed.

"You are a very clever woman, Rea-san," he said as they finally left the studio. "Professor Inariyama is a great man. The good opinion of such a man is like a treasure." He gave her a quick, beaming smile. "I am sorry Akira-san could not be here to listen to you. He, too, would have been glad for you."

Rea simply bowed. She was sure that Ivan could not have cared less about her success or failure, that he had merely sent Satoh-san with her to complete what business dealings they still had. Anyway, his approbation wasn't necessary. Jan and Tucker took care of any celebrating that had to be done, with a champagne toast that evening. They were all a little silly from their third or fourth glass of champagne when the phone rang.

This time, it was Ivan's aunt, Lady Sachiko, calling from Kyoto. "I watched you on that panel today," the elderly woman said in her lovely, muted voice. "I was very impressed! You are now so famous that you will probably not be interested in my poor company, but I would very much like to invite you to come down to Matsuyashiki this weekend. Midori will be here, as well as several other guests. Will you come?"

Rea hedged. "Your ladyship is too kind. But I don't know how to get to Pine Manor. And—"

"But that is too simple!" Lady Sachiko broke in. "My nephew will drive you down, of course. He and Midori are coming on Friday, in the late afternoon. You will come together."

"Yes, but—"

"By all means bring a nice dress with you, my dear. There will be a small party on Saturday night . . . after some entertainment." Lady Sachiko paused delicately. "I am having Yamaguchi here, you know. The Kabuki actor."

The old woman was holding a carrot in front of Rea's nose. Yamaguchi, the most famous woman-impersonator on the Kabuki stage . . . who could resist him? She could not, for one! When she hung up the phone, she was smiling ruefully.

Janet opened her eyes wide at the news. "You must be doing something right," she said. "I've been in Japan for years and years, and Lady Sachiko has never invited me to a house party!"

Tucker teased her. "Good-time Charlie, that's you . . . I thought you'd want to work, so I brought home a lot of old photos and maps I had at the office. Now they'll just have to sit around and collect dust, worse luck."

Rea burst out laughing. "You two are as bad as Lady Sachiko. One thing I've learned about this country—never argue with a woman aristocrat! She always gets her way."

Rea put off packing her things for the weekend until the last possible moment. She pretended that it was work that kept her from thinking about the trip, but actually, she did not want to think about Ivan. What would they say to each other? Her moods were like a barometer gone crazy, now glad, now miserable. But that was the way Ivan had always affected her.

When she did pack, she purposely left out the two dresses Ivan had bought for her at La Charmante. Instead, she took her old beige dress, the white cocktail dress and some jeans and T-shirts. If these weren't good enough for the guests at Matsuyashiki, she was sorry. Almost defiantly, she threw her clothes into a small suitcase Janet had lent her and shut the lid.

Ivan and Midori came for Rea a few minutes after five on Friday. Actually, it was Ivan who came to the door. He hardly looked at her as he exchanged a few words of greeting with Tucker and Janet and then offered to carry her suitcase downstairs.

"Thank you, no," Rea said calmly. "I can manage."

He stood aside to let her walk ahead of him to the elevator, and she walked briskly, careful not to show the raging emotions that had burst through her at the sight of him. He was dressed casually, in summer slacks and sports shirt, but the princely air that always characterized him was there. So was the curve of his mobile lips, the clear green eyes . . . every facet and nuance of him that she remembered. She forced herself to smile at him as they got into the elevator.

"It's kind of you to drive me to Lady Sachiko's home."

"Nonsense. Midori and I are going anyway." His speech was abrupt, and he did not look at her. "Midori is going to stay in Kyoto for some time with our aunt. I warn you that she is not very happy about the prospect and is rather moody."

Midori did not seem moody as she waved happily when she saw Rea. "Rea! I have missed you! Ivan and I saw you on TV, and we were crazy about your performance! You had all those old graybeards staring at you with their mouths open!"

Ivan was driving his Lancia, so Rea had to squeeze into the front seat with him and Midori. "You will love Matsuyashiki," Midori bubbled on. "It is a wonderful place. It even pleases my brother, who has been so grumpy lately, I am disgusted with him." In response, Ivan merely backed up the car and put it into gear. "He is angry with me because I don't want to go to Kyoto for a long visit. I prefer Osaka."

Rea was glad for Midori's chattiness. She wondered how things had gone after the *omiyai* at the exposition banquet, but didn't dare ask. "Do you visit Kyoto often?" she asked.

Midori made a face. "Often enough. My brother and my father think that a long stay with Aunt Sachi will make me behave like a Japanese *ojosan*. They think I am unladylike at present." She stuck out her tongue at her brother, who gave her a startled glare, then burst into a shout of laughter.

"Midori, you are impossible," he said. "What will Rea think of you? You have no face at all."

"I'd rather have no face than turn into a prim and proper bore like Catherina," Midori said heatedly. "I'd much rather be an old maid than marry anyone *you* and Father picked for me, too. Look at Rea. She isn't married, and she's happy in her work."

"I hardly think Rea is an old maid," Ivan said. His look at Rea was very brief, but it had all the flashing intensity of a lightning bolt. She felt a tightness in her chest, and her arms unconsciously reverted to the old hugging gesture she hated. When she realized what she was doing, she frowned and forced herself to lay her hands lightly in her lap. "You had better behave yourself," Ivan continued, speaking to Midori. "It will be a long ride."

He was right about the distance, and Rea was relieved that Midori continued talking. She began giving Rea the history of Pine Manor, telling her that it had been founded by ancestors in the seventeenth century, and she was still going on when they turned off the Meishin highway and made their way down a boulevard shaded by tall trees.

"Matsuyashiki is not far from the Kitashirakawa district," Midori was saying. "That's where most rich people build their homes, you know. It's gorgeous in the spring, Rea... covered with cherry blossoms. But Aunt Sachi's house is pretty all the time. She loves her plants and flowers and all her tall pine trees so much."

The Lancia began to climb a hill. After some time, it turned down an avenue which became a wide, graveled pathway. This pathway twisted around and turned, then led to the traditional Japanese wall. Ivan sounded his car horn, and the gateway was thrown open by an old man who nearly swept the ground with his bows.

"Welcome home . . . welcome home . . ." His face was wreathed in smiles as both Ivan and Midori shouted affectionate greetings. "Ah, you are late; we were worried about you. Her Ladyship has been watching for you for half an hour!"

"Welcome! here you are at last!" Lady Sachiko now appeared on the outer veranda that ran around the house. She held her hands out to Midori and Ivan, and somehow included Rea in this warm greeting.

"Dear children," she said. "Rea-san, I am so glad you are here. Now you must rest. For our guest, the Chrysanthemum Room has been prepared."

"The best room in the house," Midori explained, as Rea blushed to the roots of her hair, feeling Ivan's eyes on her. She knew he was remembering another chrysanthemum room. "It is much nicer than my room. The Bamboo Room, ugh! Even Ivan's Pine Room is much nicer than mine."

"It's all you deserve." Ivan laughed.

He looked different, Rea thought, watching him. His face seemed to have smoothed, become younger and much warmer. There was an eagerness in his eyes as he turned to his aunt. "We didn't eat before we left Osaka. You've prepared one of your special dinners?"

"Bad boy; we'll eat after you bathe," Lady Sachiko said. "You two children go ahead, now, and let me show our guest to her room." She nodded to one of the maids, who picked up Rea's small suitcase and proceeded into the house ahead of them. Lady Sachiko took Rea's arm. "It is a very big house for an old lady like me," she murmured confidentially. "It used to be full, you know, when my husband was alive and my younger brother, the baron, lived here with Midori and her mother. It is my hope that someday, Ivan will bring his family here to live."

Rea looked about her at the woodwork on the walls, the strips of wood interlaced to form the ceiling, the wooden hallway polished to a dull gold. The house did not look empty, as many old houses do. It had a calm, welcoming atmosphere. She mentioned it to Lady Sachiko, and the old lady smiled.

"Ah, you feel it too? It has always been a happy home, you know. After . . . his mother left, Ivan came here also. He grew up here with Midori. They filled the house with their play and their quarrels."

She slid open a paper-and-wood screen door as she spoke, and ushered Rea into a traditional Japanese room. It was about five mats large, and a handsome chrysanthemum scroll hung in the *tokonoma*. Lady Sachiko opened the screen doors overlooking the garden, and Rea caught her breath in delight. A small lily pond, stone benches and clumps of chrysanthemums in pots were hazed over by the twilight. "The chrysanthemum garden," Lady Sachiko said, pride in her voice. "I keep the flowers here even in the hottest summer. They are grown in our own greenhouses, you know. It is my hobby."

When Lady Sachiko had gone, Rea unpacked. She hung her white cocktail dress and other clothes in the closet, then stood looking out at the garden. She could imagine children being happy here . . . playing in the gardens, running down the long, polished halls. No wonder Ivan's face had lighted up on his return to Matsuyashiki. She leaned her head against the paper-and-wood screen door and wished that somewhere, a house like this existed for her. Then she shook herself free of this fancy as a maid called softly at the door that her bath was ready.

Rea enjoyed her bath—in a large old tub made of sweet-smelling wood—and went down refreshed to dinner. She found the family in a Western-style dining room, which seemed incongruous in the old Japanese house.

"This is my brother's idea of comfort," Lady Sachiko explained when Rea was seated between Ivan and Midori. "He liked to sit in a chair when he ate." However, the dinner was purely Japanese. Rea devoured every crumb of her supper . . . grilled fish, clear soup, a salad made of radishes and cucumbers, vegetables served in lovely lacquer-and-porcelain bowls. As they ate some fruit at the end of the meal, Lady Sachiko suggested that Rea might like to explore Kyoto.

"You really have all morning and afternoon to look around," she pointed out. "I am not having my guests and the Kabuki performance till around seven o'clock. There are magnificent temples in this area. The question is, which of you two will take Rea sightseeing?"

"I will, if it isn't too early," Midori said.

Ivan snorted. "That means you won't get up until noon!" He glanced at Rea, then away. "I will take you... if you wish."

Rea felt herself flushing awkwardly. However, under the eyes of Midori and Lady Sachiko, she could only nod. "That would be very kind. What time would you want to start?"

"Around five?" Ivan asked, and Midori gave a muffled moan. "It's the best time of the morning. I will take you to the Daisen temple, a Zen Buddhist temple. Sunrise there is something to experience... if you can get up at that hour."

Rea got up from the table. "In that case, I'd better get to bed early," she said. It was a perfect opportunity to escape those searching green eyes... and also to leave the little family to talk without a stranger present.

Early the next morning, when her traveler's alarm clock sounded, Rea was instantly alert and awake. She dressed quickly and went to the dining room, where she found Ivan drinking coffee. He looked up at her in surprise.

"You're up!" he exclaimed. Clearly, he had not expected her to be awake on time.

"I'm an early riser... and I love coffee in the morning, too," she said as he poured her a cup. She leaned back in her chair and sipped the hot, delicious brew. "I thought the Japanese ate a different kind of breakfast in the morning."

"Drinking coffee is a habit I got from both parents," Ivan said. He glanced at his watch. "Whenever you're ready, we can go."

Rea put down her cup and followed him as he led the way to the car. The morning was still gray, and dew lay on the courtyard. Somewhere, a bird called drowsily, and an early-morning breeze wrapped itself around Rea's shoulders like a caress. As they drove away, Rea could smell clear morning smells... pine and the mist that hung in the hills behind them. She was moved by the stillness and the peace, and glanced at Ivan to see whether he, too, felt these things. He did not return her look, and suddenly she felt ill at ease and unhappy, remembering what had happened when they were together the last time. As though he had read her mind, he said, "You know that Kyoto was once called the city of peace?" She nodded. He was silent a moment, then added, "Perhaps we, too, should call a truce. The last time we were together was . . . unfortunate." He ran a hand quickly up the back of his neck, into his dark hair. "I misread your signals, I suppose."

"Are you apologizing?" She couldn't believe that a man like Ivan ever could admit he was sorry.

He glanced at her, a quick, half-pleading, half-mocking look that made him look younger and more unsure than she had ever seen him. Then he quickly turned away. "I was proud of you on the panel discussion," he said, changing the subject. "You held your own against those savants. I did not expect you to do as well."

An old belligerence stirred in her, and she asked, sharply, "Because I am a woman?"

"Not for that reason alone. I had thought all along that your book, your work, were . . . just a pose. I think of you as too young and lovely to be called 'professor,' I suppose. But I was impressed." A warmth began to fill her as she realized he was offering her not only an apology but acceptance. The mockery with which he had so often taunted her was completely gone. As they sped along, she felt a happiness that she had never before experienced. It went beyond the senses, beyond the physical . . . though the physical was very much there, as well. Though they were separated by at least a foot, his powerfully-made, strong male body seemed very close to her. As usual, her body stirred in response to his.

"Are we close to the temple?" she asked.

"Very close. There it is now." He pulled the car to a halt, then pointed to a huge, weathered table across the deserted street. "That is the Daikokuji temple. The Daisen is inside, a temple within a temple."

He held out his hand to her, and she took it, hesitatingly. Somehow, however, the feel of his palm clasping her hand seemed right in this place. As they walked through the massive gates of the larger temple, the bells of the Daikokuji began to peal. "They are welcoming the dawn," Ivan murmured.

He led her through the temple grounds to a smaller temple

in the gardens of the great one. Here, Rea's feet crunched on gravel that had been carefully arranged to give an impression of a flowing sea. A smaller temple with polished wooden floors was before them.

"It is very old," Ivan told her. "Five hundred years, at least. The Zen Buddhists believe that this place speaks to those who will listen. I try to come here whenever I am in Kyoto."

As he spoke, the temple bells gonged again. Rea lifted her head, drinking in the peace of the temple, the cool morning air. "Look," she whispered. "The sun is rising!" Instinctively, she drew closer to Ivan, and shoulder to shoulder, they watched ribbons of color fill the sky with light.

How long they stood there, Rea did not know. It seemed only a moment before the sun burst into the sky. Ivan looked down at her, smiling. "Did the temple garden talk to you?"

"I'm not sure. I only wish I could take these moments and put them away, somehow. Don't you ever wish that, Ivan? Don't you want time to be a box into which you can put certain experiences and hold them forever?"

His hand tightened around hers. "Yes, there are times like that for me," he said quietly. "But, Rea, that is a dream. Reality is what we live by, not dreams."

She nodded, heeding his call back to the real world. Perhaps she couldn't keep hold of her dreams, either, she thought. But she was going to hold onto this moment, somehow . . . for as long as she could.

It was late in the afternoon when they returned to Pine Manor, and found Lady Sachiko busy preparing for the evening's guests. A large pavilion had been erected in the main garden of the manor, and seats had been placed before it.

"The pavilion conceals a stage," Midori explained to Rea. She looked somewhat gloomy. When Rea asked her what the matter was, she shrugged her shoulders. "I've been told that Hideo is coming tonight," she said.

"Hideo! Certainly they're not playing the *omiyai* game with you and Hideo?" Rea was surprised. Midori gave her a pitying look.

"Father and my brother have got it into their heads that

he is the right husband for me. I am disgusted with my way of life, Rea. Sometimes I want to run away," she muttered. "You were lucky. You grew up in another culture!"

Was she lucky? Rea wondered about that as she and Midori went in to bathe and dress for the evening. She thought about herself at Midori's age, going to school, working nights and weekends to pay for her master's degree, and then marrying Bill. She relived those years with him, remembering the first breathless years of her love, watched herself change from a beloved wife to one trapped in a soured marriage. Had life been easier for her than for Midori? Outwardly, at least, America was a better place for women. And yet, was life easy for women anywhere? Was she more free than Midori? One look from Ivan, and she had been almost willing to sacrifice her freedom, anything at all. She gave herself a mental shake. Better not to think of Ivan at all. Far better to accept the truce he had offered, and go on as his friend. At least now, he respected her for her brains and her work . . . and work was what she intended to concentrate on in this country.

Midori came to fetch her a few moments later. She was dressed in a stunning Dior gown, and Rea felt dowdy and underdressed beside her. Midori didn't seem aware of this, however. "First we watch the Kabuki—then we eat." She sighed. "That's Aunt Sachi's rule. The guests have already begun to arrive, so we must hurry to greet them."

The main garden had been transformed with flaring Japanese lanterns, which threw the great pines into inky relief. Lady Sachiko was greeting guests as they arrived in the garden, but Ivan came towards Rea and Midori. He complimented them on their appearance, but his eyes were on Rea as he spoke. Lady Sachiko called Midori, who hurried off, and Ivan said, "You look lovely, Rea."

His voice was warm and vibrant, like the night. A shiver rippled through her, and she lifted a hand half-unconsciously to her throat as he smiled down at her. Then he stepped away from her side and snipped a yellow chrysanthemum from one of the pots that had been placed around the garden. Wordlessly, he slid the stem of the flower in her hair, his fingers lingering against her face for a second before he moved away.

"A tribute to your beauty," he said softly.

"Why . . . thank you." Uncertainly, her lips moved in a tremulous smile. Then she struggled to regain her poise. "It's been awhile since a man offered me flowers."

Ivan was about to reply, when a request that the guests be seated came from Lady Sachiko. The Kabuki performance was about to start. Ivan slid his hand under Rea's elbow, guiding her to two seats near the front. There was the clash of wooden clappers being struck together, and then the pavilion swept open to reveal a stage.

Rea had been anxiously awaiting her first glimpse of the great Yamaguchi but hadn't known what to expect. What she saw was the stylized figure of a woman, dressed in a sweeping kimono, head coiffed in the ancient way. A man was with her. Rea gathered, through their talk and stylized gestures, that the man and woman had run away together and were on the point of a lover's suicide.

"It was very common in ancient Japan," Ivan whispered in her ear. "Suicide is still an honorable act when there is no way out of a terrible situation."

Rea watched the actors on stage, and was slowly drawn into the drama. Yamaguchi acted well, though perhaps "acted" wasn't the word. He really *was* a desperate woman, portraying agony and yet triumph as the lovers finally left the stage to go to their deaths.

The applause was loud and prolonged, and Midori appeared near Rea to ask, "Did you like it?"

"I loved it!" Rea said. Midori made a face.

"I suppose I should have enjoyed it, too, but I'm too hungry. Aunt Sachi is finally going to feed us . . . and it's a buffet. Come on, Rea, let's get something to eat!" She almost dragged Rea away from Ivan's side.

Rea was not unhappy to go. Various emotions had swept through her since Ivan had placed the flower in her hair, and she was glad to give herself time to think. However, Midori gave her no time for reflection. She handed Rea a plate and led her to a huge table spread with every imaginable delicacy. Waited on by the Matsuyashiki staff of maids, the guests were being helped to a half-Western, half-Japanese buffet. Rea found her plate heaped with sliced beef, fish, *sushi*. She could not finish it all, but Midori consumed her meal with great appetite.

"I wonder where Ivan has gone to," Midori said when her appetite had been somewhat dulled. Rea had been wondering that, too. Suddenly, she caught sight of him at the other end of the garden. He was walking towards two newly-arrived guests.

"Oh, no!" Midori groaned.

"What's the matter?" Rea asked. Then she realized who the new arrivals were. She saw Hideo . . . and with him was Catherina da Silva.

The party was a long one, lasting late into the night. By the time the last guests left, it was well past midnight. Catherina and Hideo were among the last to leave. Lady Sachiko even offered Catherina an invitation to stay the night, but she refused, saying that her father expected her at a business luncheon the next day.

Rea was glad when the guests had gone and the manor settled into silence. While the servants cleared away the chairs and cutlery, she went to her room. She was exhausted. Part of her exhaustion, she knew, came from her conflicting emotions, which had begun with Ivan's accompanying her to the Daisen temple in the morning, and had been exacerbated by Catherina's arrival. Catherina had acted like a gracious lady with her, plainly implying that it was she who someday would be the lady of Matsuyashiki. She had kept Ivan in attendance all evening, leaving Rea to speak to the neglected Hideo.

Rea had gotten to know Hideo quite well, and rather liked him. Behind his unassuming face and manner, he was well read, and had an excellent sense of humor. He also genuinely cared for Midori, and was very unhappy that she disliked him. Rea sighed as she hung up her white dress and slid on the long, soft, print *yukata,* the summer sleeping kimono, that Lady Sachiko had provided. Perhaps that was the way of the world. Lovers very seldom were made happy. Some even killed themselves, as the Kabuki actors had portrayed their lovers doing.

She lay down on her sleeping quilts but was restless. It

was hot and close in the room, and she got up to pull open the screens that looked out over the garden. A cool night breeze stirred through the chrysanthemum garden, and the moonlight reflected on the little pond was silver and gold. The pines that edged the garden were powdered with silvery moonlight, and the night scents of the garden—pine and pungent chrysanthemum and the smell of water—were borne to her on the wind.

She stepped down off the wooden veranda and walked out onto the soft gravel of the garden. The night enfolded her, and the gravel underfoot was like sand. "It's so beautiful," she said with a sigh.

"It is." She hadn't expected to hear Ivan's deep voice beside her, and she looked up, confused, a little afraid. He smiled down at her, and she realized that he, too, was dressed in a darker *yukata,* which he had belted easily around the waist. "I see that you couldn't sleep either."

"I suppose I was overexcited."

He made no move to touch her, but there was an undercurrent of tension between them, a magnetic current that seemed to flame as they faced each other. His eyes roved over her, and Rea had the sudden feeling that he was stripping away her *yukata* with those green eyes. She felt a hardening of her nipples against the cotton sleeping garment.

"You left the chrysanthemum in your hair," he said. He reached out to touch her cheek, and she shivered. "Are you cold, Rea?"

"How . . . how did you get here?" she whispered.

"My room is next to yours." He stepped closer to her, and turned her around to face him. Her breath caught in her throat at his touch, and a surge of desire swept through her . . . desire so powerful that she felt faint. "The night called you outside, didn't it?" His voice was husky with wanting her. "Look at the moon. It's a lovers' moon, Rea. . . ."

She gave a little gasp as she went into his arms, his strong, hard arms that pulled her against him. His lips were warm and demanding, parting hers, seeking the softness of her mouth, his tongue probing and caressing. He seemed a part of her, and they were both a part of the night.

His kisses became more passionate. The robe about her

waist was loosening, and she felt her naked breasts against his bare chest. "Wait," he murmured, and loosened his sash, then hers. He pulled her against him, so that they stood completely naked against each other. She felt, tasted, smelled his flesh, and it seemed as if the lean, muscular body was already a part of hers. Her brain reeled with the memory of how it had been before, that one time at the Chrysanthemum inn. She felt she would fall if she didn't cling to him.

"Ivan," she moaned. She wanted him to make love to her. She had never wanted his loving more than now. With an inarticulate groan, he bent his head to her breasts, lifting her up and off the ground so that his mouth could more easily find her nipples. One hand held her close to him; the other stroked the length of her body, smoothing over her abdomen and between her thighs. In a moment, they would make love. She wanted his love. She was stupefied, lost in her desire for this man.

And yet, something inside her made her tense within his arms, tense inside herself. She whispered, "Oh, Ivan, no . . ." and when he would not listen, grasped his head in both her hands, trying to push him away from her. "Please . . . stop!"

His voice had a dazed, husky quality. "Why? For God's sake, why? You want me. You know it would be even better than it was before for us . . ."

Yes, lovemaking would be good. Yet she knew she could not let him take her here in this moon-drenched garden. Once, she had given herself to Ivan . . . and she knew that if she went to him again, she would never want anyone else in her life afterward. Dimly, she sensed that she already loved this man a thousand times more than she had ever loved Bill. She would want all of him, for always, and that could never be. What had he himself said about dreams and reality? Tonight was a dream of passion. Reality was tomorrow . . . and Catherina . . . and the Akiras' industrial ambition.

"You knew I'd be here waiting for you." He put her away from him, frowning down into her eyes. "Why else would you have come? Forget your foolish ideas, Rea. Only remember that we are together."

He bent down to kiss her again. With a choked gasp, she tore herself from his arms and staggered backwards. Her *yukata* half slid from her shoulders, and she gathered it to her with shaking hands. "Nothing's changed between us," she whispered. "Ivan, don't you see? It wouldn't be right for me . . . or for you."

She turned and stumbled back to the screen doors of the Chrysanthemum Room. When she turned again, the garden was empty. Ivan had gone, and the moonlight sparkled down on the crushed yellow flower that had fallen from her hair.

- 11 -

"DON'T YOU HAVE an appetite this morning, Rea-san?"

"Thank you, no, Lady Sachiko." Rea pushed aside the juicy Japanese peaches Lady Sachiko had placed before her. For once, she had no appetite at all, not even for a succulent peach. She had purposely come down late so that she could avoid seeing Ivan after last night, only to learn that he had left for Osaka on some urgent company business. Lady Sachiko explained that the office chauffeur would be sent down to take Rea back that evening.

"Are you well?" The old lady eyed Rea worriedly. Rea nodded, but she didn't feel well at all. There was a tightness behind her eyes, and her head ached. She had lain awake all last night, listening to the sounds outside in the garden. Once, she thought she heard footsteps, and had sat up in her quilts . . . her gesture proving to her that if Ivan did return, she could not bear to refuse him again. But there had been no one in the chrysanthemum garden.

Lady Sachiko glanced at Midori. "This one, also, has no appetite," she said ruefully. Midori got up from the breakfast table and walked away without a word. The elderly lady sighed. "Excuse my niece, Rea-san. It is a difficult time for her." Rea murmured something. "The time between girlhood and womanhood is hard, these days," Lady Sachiko went on. "It was easier when I was a girl. I went from my father's home to my husband's, and that was the best way."

"These are modern times," Rea pointed out, but Lady Sachiko only sniffed.

"That doesn't mean anything." She turned her glittering narrow eyes to Rea. "Take you, for instance. I am a little concerned about you. I hear your parents are dead." Rea nodded, a little amused at the old lady's brisk tone. "Who undertakes to see that you are happily married?" Lady Sachiko demanded.

"No one. In the West—"

"I know that you choose your own mates. However, this is not always wise. I admire your work exceedingly, but are you happy? Forgive me, but you are over thirty, I think."

Rea noted the real concern in the old lady's voice and could not feel indignant. Lady Sachiko shook her head sadly. "You would be such a lovely wife and mother," she said, sighing. "You would have splendid children."

"Right now, my book and my career are home and children to me," Rea said.

"So. Your work is everything to you. You are like my nephew. I worry about him also," Lady Sachiko said, crinkling her eyebrows. "He thinks about nothing but his work. He has no outside interests that matter. I sometimes am fearful for him."

"Afraid *for* him?" Rea asked, and Lady Sachiko nodded.

"Does that sound strange? He seems strong and sure of himself, like one of my great pines, but you know what happens to tall trees in a storm. They fall, Rea-san . . . they do not have resilience. I think it is because his mother went away when he was little. You know about this?"

"I have heard a little," Rea said doubtfully.

"That was a sad thing. My brother adored his Golden Rose, and she was a good woman . . . and she loved him. In the end, she went away for his sake. She left because she knew her staying would cause a rift in the Akira family." She paused. "You do not understand?"

"She did leave her son," Rea said carefully. "Why didn't she take Ivan with her?"

"For my brother's sake, again. And she refused anything . . . money, jewels, property. She did not tell my brother where she went, Rea-san. He searched for years! Once in a while, he got news of her, and finally he learned that she was dead."

"And . . . Ivan?"

Lady Sachiko sighed. "He doesn't speak of her very

much. But . . . for many months after he came to Matsuyashiki, his pillow was damp with tears in the morning." She got to her feet. "Have you ever seen a photograph of Alexandra?"

"No," Rea said. Lady Sachiko made a beckoning gesture.

"I keep the photograph in my room," she said. "I have kept it all these years, because I always liked her. If you come with me, I will show it to you."

Lady Sachiko's room was called the Peony Room, and overlooked a serene stretch of white sand dotted with clumps of peonies. "This is the finest room in the house," she said. "From it, you can see the moon rise every night. It gives a calmness to the spirit, Rea-san." She went to a closet with a sliding door, pulled out a drawer and drew out a photograph in a silver frame. She handed the photograph to Rea, who looked down on a blond woman in evening dress.

"You see how pretty she was," Lady Sachiko said.

Rea nodded, though she felt that 'pretty' was too nice a word. Alexandra had a strong face, too full of character to be called merely pretty. Her hair was very fair, and though she could not tell from the black-and-white photograph, Rea was sure her eyes were as green as Ivan's. She wore no jewelry except a small ring on one finger.

"I wish I could have known her," she found herself saying.

Unexpectedly, Lady Sachiko nodded. "So do I. She would have liked you." She took the photograph from Rea and held it at arm's length, looking at it.

Why was Lady Sachiko telling her all this? Rea wondered. Perhaps she was telling her that her situation with Ivan reminded her of the sad story of the Golden Rose. Perhaps she had seen them together in the chrysanthemum garden. . . .

The memory of last night brought a flush to Rea's cheeks, and she hastily turned from the elderly woman to admire the garden. She felt the touch of Lady Sachiko's hand on her arm.

"Someday, you must come back to Matsuyashiki and share a moonrise with me, Rea-san," she said. "I will offer you tea and rice cakes. Alexandra and I did this often together, you know. I would be glad to share my garden and my moon with you also."

Rea returned to Osaka that evening, and work occupied her for the next weeks. June slid into July almost imperceptibly, except that the rainy season made the heat worse. Sometimes, Rea was caught in a sudden thunderstorm as she traveled around Osaka, using the bus system, for she had learned to understand it. She also grew familiar with the railway system, traveling by way of Hanshin railway to Kobe, or on to Nara. She found that her travels gave her a better, clearer knowledge of the Japanese . . . students, railway conductors, shopkeepers. She also attended several of Professor Inariyama's lectures at Osaka University, and had many long conversations with him. Yet the one man she most wanted to see and hear from never came near her.

She told herself that she was glad, that she would not see him even if he did come to her. But wherever she went, a remembered curve of cheek, a sudden gesture from some complete stranger, would send her mind spinning and reeling to that moon-drenched summer's night in the garden. In her dreams, he came too, sliding the *yukata* from her eager body, drawing her against his demanding maleness. Outwardly, she had forgotton him. Inwardly, she drew the moments shared with him, the memory of his face and the smell of him and the touch of his skin, into a secret compartment of her heart.

One morning at breakfast, Tucker mentioned that Ivan's name had figured in the news. "Seems your old friends the Akiras are going to be busy," he said. "The Bamboo Baron just got the contract he wanted with those American concerns we talked about. You probably helped them, Rea, by entertaining that Jim Hume."

Rea made a noncommittal sound, and saw Janet glance up at her with a suddenly worried look. She had seen Janet's concern from time to time since her return from Matsuyashiki. All Janet said, however, was, "Are you doing anything special today?"

"Osaka Castle," Rea said. Both the Wynns groaned.

"Honey, the castle is *the* hottest place in Osaka," Tucker protested. "That huge park . . . and all those white stones."

"And it's not even historic," Janet added. "You know it was built after the war."

Rea explained that the modernity of the castle was what she found so interesting. "I want to contrast the 'new' castle with the historical castle built back in the fifteen-hundreds," she explained. "I'm going to try to get there by bus, too . . . so wish me luck."

She set out after breakfast but soon realized that trying to get to the castle by bus was a mistake. The Japanese bus system was complex, and noon found her, lost, in a small noodle shop in some obscure corner of Osaka. While she was eating her lunch of noodles and fried prawns, several university students approached her and offered suggestions.

"Osaka Castle? It is impossible to get there by bus . . . too difficult!" one of them said when she had explained her problem. "I would take a taxi. The cost can't be too much . . . perhaps two thousand yen."

About ten dollars. Rea sighed. No matter how carefully she hoarded her resources, she was always spending money in Japan. Hearing her sigh, the students offered more suggestions, and ended up sharing lunch with her. They were well-meaning and friendly, and Rea, in chatting with them, forgot the time. When she next looked at her wristwatch, it was almost three.

She hailed a taxicab outside the noodle shop and gave the driver directions. The driver, a silent, truculent type, sped through Osaka, and Rea held her breath as she watched the meter creep up. Finally, they arrived at a broad road which bordered a park. In the distance, she could see Osaka Castle.

Wordlessly, the cab driver pulled his vehicle to a halt, and Rea fumbled in her purse for her wallet. Then her heart nearly stopped. The wallet wasn't there! Frantic now, she searched again. When she couldn't find it, she tried to remember when she'd last used it. She had paid for her meal at the noodle shop. Could she have left it there? Probably. But now, how was she to pay the cab driver?

He was staring at her in a suspicious way. When she explained the situation, he frowned. "What are you trying to do?" he demanded. "You're trying to cheat an honest man!"

"I'm very sorry. I left my wallet at the shop..." Rea fought for calm, which was not easy, in light of the belligerent look in the man's eyes.

"You pay up, or I'll call the police," the driver threatened. "I know you foreigners!"

Rea calmed herself with an effort. She would telephone Tucker or Janet... they'd somehow get to her and bail her out of this jam. "I will telephone my friends," she told the angry man. "They will bring the money to us."

"There is no telephone here!"

Rea looked around her. The wide park was empty. Further on, however, by the castle moat, Rea spied a few small souvenir stands. She told the driver she would go there and ask about a phone, and he growled that he would follow her. With the driver walking threateningly behind her, Rea hurried across the hot grass.

The souvenir stands were even smaller than Rea had thought, and there was no phone. "Perhaps there is one at the school, near the castle," one of the stall-keepers said.

Before the cab driver could argue, Rea began hurrying across the moat and up a long, twisting path. Pebbles were underfoot, and one of them slipped, causing Rea to twist her ankle badly. The pain shot up her ankle and into her knee, but Rea bit her lip and disregarded it. Hobbling a little, she continued up the path and then over a flight of stone steps.

After an eternity of more twisted pathway, a building came into sight. Rea could see boys, some as little as five or six years of age, dressed in Japanese costumes with wooden staves over their shoulders. This was a *kendo* school, where Japanese martial arts were taught. Rea hailed one of the youngsters and asked if there was a phone in the school.

With the cab driver breathing down her neck, Rea followed the surprised youngster into the school. There, mercifully, was a phone. After asking for permission to use it, Rea dialed the *Outlook* office, only to be told Tucker was out. She had no luck at Janet's clinic, either, for Janet was out on an emergency visit to the hospital.

There was only one other person she could call. She

drew a deep breath, then dialed Akira Industries. She asked for Satoh-san, but the voice that answered her call was not Mr. Satoh's.

"Akira here," the voice said.

Rea's voice shook in spite of herself. "Ivan? Ivan, I'm so sorry to trouble you, but I'm in a difficult situation . . ."

"Rea?" Incredulity replaced his usual crispness. "What's the matter?" Ivan asked. He listened to her explanations, then added, "Let me talk to the cab driver."

If her ankle had not been so sore, Rea would have laughed at the change that came over the man. He took the phone receiver suspiciously, and then an astonished look filled his small eyes. His voice changed, as well, and he snapped to attention and began to bow deeply. *"Hai!"* he exclaimed. "Yes, sir, yes! Yes, your honor . . . immediately!" Reverently, he handed the phone back to Rea. "He wishes to talk to you, madam."

"What did you say to him?" Rea asked Ivan, in English.

"It doesn't matter. You are at the castle? Enjoy yourself there. When you have finished, take a taxi back to the Wynns' apartment and use my firm's name. I will take care of this man."

"But Ivan . . ." a whirring sound on the other end told her that he had severed the connection. She looked from the receiver to the cab driver, somewhat troubled. Instantly, the man began to bow again, his face now a mass of smiles.

"Please do not trouble yourself, honored lady," he said, and then frowned at several of the *kendo* school students who had gathered around, grinning and giggling and enjoying the show. "I will depart now, with your permission." As she watched, he bowed himself out of sight.

Rea thanked the school officials, then hobbled out into the harsh July afternoon. She hesitated, wondering whether she should go back at once. Her foot was very sore . . . and yet, she had come all this way. She might at least take some photographs of the castle. Limping along, she walked up the pathway and through a fence, which widened into an enclosure around the castle gate and the castle itself. Rea's throat was burning with thirst, but although there were restaurants around the enclosure, she had no money. Gritting her teeth against the pain and her thirst, she took photographs until the pain in her leg made it impossible to walk or stand. Then she hobbled through the enclosure and happened onto a Japanese garden at the foot of the castle gate. Gratefully, she sank onto the grass beside a pond banked by bushes of summer flowers. Stretching her throbbing leg in front of her, she pulled out her notebook and began to jot down impressions.

Once having begun to write, she forgot the time. Her mind returned to the original castle, constructed in the sixteenth century and brought to its knees less than a hundred years later. What blood must have been shed here, she thought. What archers must have stood behind the slatted windows, pouring rivers of arrows onto besieging armies! She put down her pen and stared at the high tower, glistening in the sun.

"They say that each night of the last siege, a lone samurai played his reed flute to mock the besiegers," a voice said behind her, and Ivan sat down beside her on the grass. "In those days, this was a fortification . . . the guardian of the city. A good place to live . . . a fine place to die."

She stared at him. "How did you get here so fast?"

"How do you think? I drove, of course! I realized that you must have no money and couldn't even get into the castle."

She was completely speechless as he looked up at her, his green eyes half closed against the late-afternoon sun. "I . . . I must repay you," she said uncertainly.

"Must you always talk about money? Right now, I thought you would want to see the castle before they close the gates."

Rea got to her feet, then winced with pain. "What's the matter?" Ivan asked sharply. "Are you hurt? Did that damned cab driver—"

"No. No, I twisted my ankle a little. It's all right," Rea said. She tried to smile, but pain pulled her lips into a grimace.

"You should go home immediately and soak that foot," he said sternly. Kneeling down, he took her foot in his hands, and moved it gently. "Does this hurt?"

"No," she said, acutely aware of his warm, sure hands on her leg. How gently he held her foot in his hands, and how the gentleness contrasted with the rest of his appearance. Kneeling as he did, she had the impression of leashed power emanating from him.

"Nothing seems broken, but I think you need to rest it, after all. You can see the castle another day."

He slid an arm around her to support her, and the thrill of his nearness ran through her like a slow electric charge. Slowly, they walked through the garden and out of the gate. He held her close to his side, and she had a great urge to lay her cheek against the support of his shoulder. As they stepped outside the fence, Ivan nodded to a group of large boulders.

"Those are perhaps more worth seeing than the castle itself," he said. "Those stones are part of the old Osaka Castle. They were dragged out of the Inland Sea long ago, hauled into rafts and lugged up here to be the base of the castle. Come and touch them, Rea. Then you can truly say you've touched history."

He guided her to the great stones, and she leaned against them, running her hands over their surface, warm from the sun. She frowned in concentration, trying to think of the people who had lived at the base of the old castle. Shadowy old warriors and peasants and merchants and courtesans . . . lovers, perhaps, who were now dust.

In his uncanny way of reading her mind, Ivan said, "The moon looked down on those people long ago . . . the sun beat down on them. They all lived and died near these old stones! He drew her close to him again as they resumed walking, and he bent his lips so that they touched her ear. "A place to love and a place to die."

If she turned a little, she would be in his arms. He still wanted her . . . that much she could guess. That she wanted him, she knew. Blood surged through her at his nearness, and she felt with every pore and cell of her body the warmth of his skin beneath the cotton shirt he wore, the aching need of that flesh.

"We'd better be getting back," she said, and her voice was almost steady. "I'm so grateful for your being here,

Ivan, but now I think you're right. I'd better get back to the Wynns' and soak my ankle."

Rea was half afraid that the Wynns might be home when Ivan helped her up to the apartment door. She did not relish having to explain, or of seeing that probing look Janet had been giving her lately. She was also grateful when Ivan left her at the door, making no move to follow her in. She knew that a word from her would have precipitated the same kind of situation as the one in the chrysanthemum garden, and she was relieved when he left her with no more than a perfunctory goodbye.

Inside the apartment, she took off her stockings and examined her ankle. As Ivan had said, it did not appear broken, and she found an ace bandage of Jan's which would do until the doctor returned. She then settled down to her writing . . . the only cure for her now-turbulent thoughts. She was deep in the history of Osaka Castle when the doorbell rang. She looked up, annoyed, and glanced at her wristwatch. It was too early for either of the Wynns to return, and anyway, why would they be ringing their own doorbell? Hobbling, she walked to the door.

"Who is it?" she asked, irritated anew by a second, even more impatient ring of the bell.

"Akira." A tumult of emotions raced through her . . . dismay, confusion, joy. She hesitated, and he said, "Open the door, Rea. There's no use trying to hide anything."

"Hide? What on earth . . ." She pulled the door open, and he strode past her into the apartment. "What are you doing?"

"Midori. Where is she?" Ivan demanded.

"Why should I know where she is?" Surprised and indignant, Rea protested as Ivan walked through the Wynns' bedroom and then stalked into hers. He slid open her closet door, while she demanded, "How dare you? What are you doing?"

"I was sure she was here." He was frowning, his face taut with anger. "She disappeared today from Matsuyashiki. My aunt telephoned while we were at the castle."

"And you thought she'd come here to me?"

"Aunt Sachi said she might have confided in you. You were on good terms, and you would be sympathetic to her, having the mistaken impression that she was a badly-treated young woman."

"Would you like to search under the bed?" she demanded, then flushed deeply as he glanced at her bed and back at her in a way that made his thoughts very obvious. "Perhaps you'll be good enough to get out of my room!" she cried.

"Can't you see how serious this is?" he snapped at her. "Midori has actually run away from our aunt. She left a note saying she'd be back only when we allowed her to be a free woman. If word of this leaks out, it'll be bad for the family."

"And you would lose face?" Because she felt so confused, she took refuge in baiting him. "I suppose you haven't thought that you could consider Midori's feelings!"

He turned towards her, eyes glittering through narrowed lids. "So. I was right, wasn't I? You'd encourage her disobedience . . ."

"Disobedience? She's a human being, not a . . . a dog! Yes, I'd encourage it. If I knew where she was, I wouldn't tell you!"

He reached out and grabbed her by the shoulders, his fingers hurtful. She wasn't sure whether he was going to hit her or not, and she didn't care. All her pent-up emotions came crowding into her throat, making it hard for her to speak. "You make me ill, Ivan Akira. You think that all you need do is to snap your fingers and a woman will do as you want. Disobedience! Oh, you egotistical, self-centered . . . bully!"

"Are you finished?" He let go of her and began to walk to the door.

"No, I haven't! Don't you dare walk away from me. . . ." She grabbed his arm as she spoke, and he moved so swiftly, she gasped. In a second, they were in direct confrontation, his face inches from hers. She had never seen him so angry.

"Tell me what else you have to say." His voice was quiet, but she felt as if she had been slapped. She tried to break loose from him, but he was too strong, and she could only turn away her head as the first sob errupted from deep within her.

He didn't let her go, but his touch changed. As her other sobs came, he drew her into his arms, holding her tightly against him. Through her tears, she felt his hands stroking her hair, cradling her. "Go away!" she sobbed in humiliation. "Please . . . just go!"

He paid no attention, but scooped her into his arms and sat down with her on the narrow bed, rocking her in his arms as if she were a child. "Dear little one," he whispered, "don't cry. I didn't mean to hurt you. *Duschenka,* don't cry."

He drew her head against his chest, and she felt his lips touch her forehead, her cheek, cool lips that were suddenly warm as they reached her mouth. The terrible, hard pain inside her changed, released itself into a languid, sensual warmth that spread through her. She knew that if she were to pull herself away from him now, he would let her go. She did not want to move away from him. She could no more will herself to leave the comfort and strength of his arms than she could stop herself from lifting her wet face so that he could kiss her eyelids, and then her tremulous lips. For a moment, the warm kiss was gentle . . . and then she felt her own urgency mount as his lips parted hers.

A low moan escaped from her. He was unbuttoning her blouse, loosening the garment from around her shoulders. Next, her skirt. Her own fingers eagerly reached out to unbutton his shirt, to run fingers over the smooth, warm skin of his muscular chest. He lay her back down on the bed and slid away her brassiere, kissing her breasts before moving his lips downward. She felt the rasp of his cheek against her abdomen, and then the touch of his mouth moving lower. Rea closed her eyes. It was a current in which they were both caught, a current that was taking them far out to sea. He was water and she moonlight, and they were a part of each other. Why fight the tug of passions that tormented them both? She wrapped her fingers in his dark hair, tugging him gently back to her so that they could kiss each other hungrily.

Between kisses, he undressed. There were no words between them—there was no need of words. In a moment, they would be together. This second lovemaking they had both wanted so long . . . why had she fought against such unbearable rapture? An unformed thought was creeping into her pleasure-drenched brain . . . and she pushed it away. But the thought came anyway. Today you'll make love with him, Rea. What about tomorrow?

Nothing had changed, not really. Ivan wanted her, but she wanted more than physical coupling. Even though her body ached with the same desire that filled him, she must stop this—stop it now, while she could still bear to do so.

"Ivan," she whispered. "Wait!"

"No more waiting, Rea. Not now," he replied huskily.

"But you have to. I . . . I can't let us do this."

He suddenly tensed beside her. "What kind of game are you playing?"

"It's not a game for me!" Her lips felt bruised, and so did her heart as she forced the words from herself. He'd never know how much each word cost her! "I want you very much, Ivan, but I—it wouldn't be enough just to sleep with you. I would want too much . . . and it just isn't possible. Far better not to start."

"We've already started." He reached for her again, but she pushed his hands away determinedly. "You really mean it," he said incredulously.

She pulled herself away from him, reaching for the bedcover, which she wound around her breasts and hips. "I'm going to leave Japan in a month or so," she said slowly. "I have my work and . . . and my own life. So do you. I can't just give myself to you for a few hours or a few days and then . . . go away and forget you."

He smiled suddenly, the tension easing from his face. "Then stay here with me! Is that what worries you? I can take an apartment for us. Whatever you want, Rea. You know I'm crazy about you . . ."

"You haven't listened to me! I have my work. It's important to me," she whispered. "Being your mistress wouldn't be enough for me, Ivan."

Gradually, the eagerness in his eyes died. The old hard shell of mockery descended over his face. "So," he said, and was quiet for a moment. Then he laughed, without humor. "All this foreplay was perhaps in the way of research? The sex patterns of the modern executive, perhaps?"

"Ivan." She couldn't stand the look in his eyes, so she turned away. She could hear him dressing, but stayed where she was, quiet, unmoving. He was leaving her, she thought miserably. He did not understand her. How could he, when she barely understood herself? Part of her wanted to throw her arms around him, beg him to make love to her, keep her for as long as he wanted, any way he wanted. But the memory of Bill stopped her. Never again would she go to a man on his terms.

He was dressed. She sensed it before she turned to him, saw him standing on the threshold of her room. "You had better dress before your friends return," he said, urbane as ever. He pulled down the cuffs of his shirt and smiled at her, the upturned mockery of his lips not able to hide the bitterness in his eyes. "If Midori telephones you, by the way, you had best advise her to return to her family. I think that any normal woman would prefer a man in her bed to the cold comfort of a life of writing books and teaching other people's children."

She couldn't answer him. He turned away from her, and spoke without looking at her. "*Sayonara,* Professor Rea Harley," he said.

- 12 -

REA FILLED HER days with work. Tucker read part of her first draft, and declared, "This isn't just for scholars—it's good reading, Rea! I'd send a copy to Professor Inariyama at Osaka University. He'd be interested in what you're doing."

Rea finally agreed, and two days after she mailed the material, the famous educator telephoned Rea. Enthusiastic, he had valuable suggestions, and he even opened the library and facilities of his university to her.

He also let her use his private collection of books, and they had several discussions that Rea found invaluable. It was Inariyama who told her about the *Tanabata* Festival, the celebration of the Celestial Lovers.

"It will be tomorrow night," he told Rea one afternoon. "Are you going to celebrate with your friends?"

"I hadn't thought about it." Rea knew about *Tanabata;* the folktale had been one of her favorites. It concerned a romance between Vega and Altair, two stars separated through the long year but permitted to meet on July seventh. "I always thought *Tanabata* was for children."

But when she returned home, the Wynns were in a state of excitement. Lady Sachiko had telephoned while Rea was at the university. "She wants the three of us to join in a *Tanabata*-night dinner," Janet told Rea enthusiastically. "They will all be going to a large restaurant in town. You'll like it, Rea. Lady Sachiko always does things in a big way."

"Did you say I would go?" Rea asked sternly. Jan shook her head.

"No, but Tucker and I are going to go. It will do you

good, Rea, after working so hard. You know the old saying about all work and no play."

But Rea was adamant in refusing. Janet didn't press her, and Rea was relieved. She telephoned at once to Lady Sachiko, conveying her regrets, and helped her friend choose a dress for the dinner. She made Janet promise to give her a detailed report on the party. "Tell Midori 'hello' for me," she added. "See how she's been since that wretched business. You know, of her running away from home after the *omiyai*.. I wonder if she and Hideo are still being thrown together."

"I doubt it," Jan replied. "Midori's an Akira. Akiras usually get their way in the end."

But Akiras didn't always get their own way! Rea thought of Ivan momentarily, remembering vividly his tall, powerful grace . . . the touch of his mouth on hers. She bit her lip and told herself to forget it. Ivan had probably long since forgotton about her in the arms of some other woman. And there was Catherina . . . No. Far better that she forget all about Ivan Akira.

The day of the *Tanabata* Festival dawned cloudy and humid, and showers were forecast. There was even more of a threat of rain that evening, and Janet began to debate whether or not to wear the costume she'd chosen. She was thinking it over when the phone rang.

Tucker groaned. "Just our luck . . . some patient or other. Damn, there goes the doorbell. I have to hurry and change. Rea, answer it, will you?"

Yet when Rea asked who the caller was, the answering voice made her stiffen. Then she composed herself. Tucker and Jan were Lady Sachiko's guests. Why shouldn't Ivan come for them? With outward calm, she opened the door.

"Good evening." He did not smile, but his eyes moved over her with a swift thoroughness that made her acutely aware of their last meeting and the fact that she had lain naked in his arms. His eyes told her that he remembered every curve and hollow of her body. Her cheeks flamed as she tried to speak lightly.

"The Wynns will soon be ready. Won't you sit down? Would you like something to drink?"

"Thank you, no. There'll be enough to drink at the restaurant. My aunt and sister are sorry, by the way, that you are not joining us. Aunt Sachi was looking forward to seeing you again."

The expression in his eyes made her turn away from him. A sudden sense of loss stabbed through her, and she found herself wrapping her arms about herself again in that old, weak gesture. "I'm very sorry," she said, in a muted voice. "My work . . . it keeps me busy."

"So I hear. Professor Inariyama is an old friend of the family. He was very impressed with you." Before he could speak again, Tucker hurried into the room. He looked upset.

"I'm very sorry, but neither Jan nor I will be able to go with you tonight," he said. "There's been a bad accident on Midosuji, and one of the victims was a patient of Jan's. She's going to the hospital now, and I'm going to go with her. I don't know what I'll be able to do except offer moral support, but . . ." He turned to Rea. "You've got to go and represent us at the party tonight."

Rea's eyes opened wide. "But I can't . . ."

"It would be really rude for none of us to go, after Lady Sachiko went to all this trouble!" Tucker said. He turned and hurried back to the master bedroom, shouting over his shoulder, "Please give her our excuses, Mr. Akira. Another time . . ."

Rea couldn't face Ivan. There was a short silence, and then she heard him laugh, a soft, rueful laugh. "There's not much you can do except come with me. You had better hurry and get dressed. We mustn't keep the others waiting."

Rea still hesitated, but Jan called her at that moment. Jan looked so anxious about her patient that Rea hadn't the heart to contradict her when the older woman took it for granted Rea was going to the party. She went to her room and stood for a second before her mirror, staring at the wide-eyed, confused face reflected there. There was fear in the wide hazel eyes, and also a hint of joy. In spite of everything, she was glad to see Ivan again. In spite of everything . . . !

Rea dressed quickly in her white cocktail outfit, and as swiftly applied eye makeup and lipstick. She was through with her preparations in five minutes, and Ivan looked genuinely surprised as she came into the living room, where he waited. His other women, Rea thought wryly, must take hours with their toilette! "Shall we go?" she asked briskly.

He bowed, with his usual mocking smile. "I am at your service, professor." He held open the door for her and as she passed him, reached out to tuck back a tendril of her hair. She ignored the storm that even this casual touch could induce in her. "I'm afraid," he went on, "that it's turned quite cloudy, and it might even rain. Bad luck for the Celestial Lovers."

"Why is that?" she asked, struggling to remain aloof as she stepped into the elevator with him. She didn't dare look at him.

"The way I heard it as a boy, the lovers can't meet if it rains. Apparently, birds form a bridge across the Milky Way in the sky so Vega and Altair can cross the starry river and meet. No birds like to fly in the rain."

Rea heard a distinct rumble of thunder as she stepped outside the apartment. Ivan's car glittered palely in the reflected light of the apartment parking lot. "Watch out for the bamboos," he told her as she was about to get into the car. "They're lying on the seat."

"You've decorated bamboo for *Tanabata!*" Rea forgot her distress momentarily, feeling pleasure as she picked up the delicate branches of Japanese bamboo, festooned with tiny paper cutouts and paper ribbons. Ivan nodded wryly.

"Midori can be a child, at times. She insisted on making the *Tanabata* bamboo . . . and later she'll insist on our casting them into some river or other. For luck."

Rea held the bamboo pieces in her lap as they drove. It was slow going, since many people in the city seemed to be out celebrating the festival. While they were driving, Rea spotted a shrine. Many people, including whole families of parents, grandparents and tiny children in kimonos, seemed headed for the shrine.

"Do you want to join them?" Ivan asked, as usual divining her thoughts.

"Could we?" Tonight, Rea wanted people around her . . . plenty of people! Perhaps numbers could exorcise the tumult she felt as she sat beside Ivan. "I suppose they are asking for a blessing," she went on. "Could a foreign woman also ask for a blessing at the shrine?"

"It depends. Blessings are like wishes. Sometimes they are given . . . sometimes not." His hand brushed her arm, and she shivered. "All right . . . I'll try to park, and we can join the shrine-goers."

He didn't touch her again after they had finally found a parking spot along the narrow road and were walking to the shrine. Rea looked around her enthusiastically. She'd been to many shrines since her arrival in Japan, but the night somehow lent magic to the huge red *torii,* the temple gate that purified the body and soul of all who passed beneath it. Besides, there was the excitement of being a part of the large group of people who climbed the flight of steep stone stairs to reach the shrine. The people waited their turn patiently, never pushing or complaining, as they approached the dark wooden shrine, step by step. Once at the top of the stairs, Ivan and Rea placed palm against palm and bowed deeply to the shadowy figures within the sanctuary. Then, carefully, they clapped their hands three times.

"You know," Rea said to Ivan as they walked down the stairs, "I was surprised when I first went through that ritual. I thought . . . that's all there is to it? But it's appropriate, isn't it? All these happy families asking a blessing of the shrine . . . and the simple, happy ritual." She was aware that he was looking down at her, and glanced up at him. Even in the darkness, the expression on his face troubled her.

"Did you ask for a blessing?" he asked. She nodded. She was not sure, but it seemed as if his voice had changed, become somehow determined. Then he said, "The restaurant where my family is waiting is in Ashiya. If we are going to be on time, we had better hurry."

Lady Sachiko and Midori greeted her with surprise and pleasure. "I was distressed when I learned you wouldn't come tonight," Lady Sachiko said as she sat Rea next to her at the traditional low Japanese table that seated Midori, Hideo and several others whom Rea did not know. "You must eat a lot, Rea-san. You have grown thin since I saw you at Matsuyashiki."

"Aunt always fusses when I lose an ounce," Midori said

with a twinkle to Rea, who saw that the young woman and Hideo were not any better friends. Midori merely ignored her suitor. "You mustn't let her bully you." The talk became general after that, and between answering questions about her book and eating the delicious food, Rea managed to keep herself from looking at Ivan. She continued to be aware of him, however, especially when Midori said, "I heard about your trip to Osaka Castle . . . and the awful taxi driver. Ivan told us all about it."

"What a terrible experience for you," Lady Sachiko agreed.

Rea found herself glancing at Ivan as they spoke, and saw that he was watching her. The intensity of that green gaze made a tightness come into her chest and throat, and it was with great difficulty that she smiled at the Akira women. Mercifully, the talk changed again, turning to the da Silvas, who, Midori said, were in Matsumoto.

"They are busy with their summer house, although Catherina is due to return to Osaka," she said. "Ivan helped design that house, so it's sure to be quite a nice one. I hope you'll get a chance to see it completed before you leave, Rea."

"Since I leave next month, I doubt that will be possible," Rea said. Catherina's name reminded her of the realities of the situation. Quite steadily, now, she returned Ivan's look. "I am sure it will be a lovely summer home," she went on. "Ivan is a fine architect, from what I've seen of the office building."

Rea did not linger after the dinner. She explained that she was tired and needed to be up early to work. Ivan offered to drive her home, and she accepted, even though she knew it was the nearness to Ivan that had produced the exhausting tension she felt. After many goodbyes and thanks, they left the restaurant. The night was as warm as bathwater, and about as humid. A sudden gash of lightning split the sky, and a thunderous peal followed.

Rea was about to get into Ivan's car, when she exclaimed out loud, "The *Tanabata* bamboos . . . we left them in the car! After all the trouble Midori took to decorate them!"

"It is a shame," Ivan agreed. "Supposing we stop on the

way and throw them into a river? Then all ceremonies will have been observed."

Just then, another stab of electricity made Rea gasp. "Are you afraid of lightning?" he asked her. "It can't hurt you. You're safe."

The way he said those words made sudden tears leap to her eyes. Had she ever been safe from harm? Resolutely, she gathered the bamboo pieces in her arms. "Where will we find a river? The Ashiyagawa?"

"Too far away. But I do know a smaller stream that would serve the purpose." Ivan slowed the car as he spoke, and pulled to the side of the road. "Over there . . . see?"

Another arc of lightning illuminated the curve of a stone bridge. Rea and Ivan got out of the car and walked towards it, each carrying a branch of bamboo. "What do we do?" Rea asked, looking down at the swirl of inky water beneath her.

"Just throw the bamboo in. Make a wish, if you like." Rea closed her eyes, as she remembered doing as a child, and made her wish when she tossed the delicate branch into the waters. She watched it whirl downstream and sighed. "My wish will probably never come true," she said. Ivan looked at her questioningly. "I wished for happiness."

He did not laugh or mock her. Instead, he reached for her hand and held it lightly in his. "Happiness can mean many things, Rea. Creativity . . . or challenge . . . or a small home overlooking a garden of flowers." He turned to her, and she tensed at the low vibrancy of his voice. "I hope you get your wish."

At that moment, the heavens opened up. Raindrops the size of grapes came splattering down on them. The summer storm, complete with thunder and bright white spears of lightning, had broken! "Shall we run to the car?" Rea gasped.

"No . . . come on! I know where there's shelter." Holding her hand, Ivan ran with an easy, long-legged stride. Rea was out of breath as he pulled her down the street. She was completely soaked, and gusts of wind made her shiver in the sudden coolness.

"Where are we going?"

"We're almost there!" Ivan ducked down a side street, and Rea sensed that there was something familiar about the doorway into which he dragged her. It was the teahouse . . . the Chrysanthemum teahouse!

"We can at least get some hot tea here, wait out the rain," Ivan explained. Rea, though hesitant, felt chilled, and followed Ivan down the corridor and into a small room.

There, a little maid clicked her tongue. "You are soaked through, madam!" she exclaimed. "You will catch a very bad cold in that wet dress." She pattered to a closet and pulled it open, revealing *yukata* and folding sleeping quilts. "Change into a *yukata,* and have a bath," she urged. "In the meantime, I will dry the dress for you in the clothes dryer."

Surprised that the little inn owned so modern a convenience, Rea did not refuse the offer at once. When she thought about it, it made sense. A hot bath . . . and a dry dress. She thought about them longingly. Besides, while she was doing all this, she would be away from Ivan's disturbing company. He nodded at her encouragingly.

"Go ahead. I couldn't face Aunt Sachi if you came down with pneumonia." Another gust of wind shuddered through the room, and Rea made up her mind.

"If you don't mind," she said apologetically to Ivan. "A hot bath does sound wonderful."

Guided by the little maid, she walked down the long corridor of polished wood until they reached a large wooden door. *"Ofuro,"* the woman said, sliding open the door to reveal a sunken tub the size of a small swimming pool. Wooden buckets stood around the tub, and a large tiled area had been set aside for bathers to wash and rinse themselves before soaking in the steaming water. The water looked wonderful!

"I will keep the other guests away while you bathe," the maid told Rea with an understanding smile, then bowed and hurried away. Rea piled her hair on top of her head, securing it with a hairpin. Then she rinsed and washed herself, and slid into the tub.

The warm water received her tenderly, and she found herself relaxing completely. "Wonderful," she murmured, eyes closed. It was purest luxury to be allowed this enormous tub to herself, to feel the heat soak through to her tired bones. "It's just marvelous," she said, again aloud.

"I told you it would be a good idea."

Rea opened her eyes and turned her head quickly. Ivan was standing by the wooden door. He was dressed in a *yukata* and was untying the sash around his waist.

"What are you doing here?" Rea gasped.

"I am about to take a bath," was the calm reply. "What do you think I'm doing? I'm as cold as you were."

"Then I'll get out and let you have the tub," Rea said firmly. She averted her eyes as he tossed aside his cotton garment and came towards the bathtub, yet she could see enough of his splendid, powerful male body to make her heart begin to pound.

"Don't be ridiculous. Don't you know Japanese bathe together? When I was at Harvard, every man and woman I met asked me about Japanese mixed bathing. It's a national obsession." She heard the splashing of water as he washed himself. "You can't go back to America without experiencing it for yourself."

Rea started to get out of the tub, but stopped herself as he slid into the water beside her. The large tub seemed suddenly crowded as he filled it with his overpowering maleness. Quietly, he said, "Why all this modesty, Rea? You've seen me before . . . and I've seen you without clothes on." She glanced at him quickly, and saw him watching her with his head to one side. The heat and the water had made his dark hair curl at the ends, and the bath water rippled against his broad chest. She could not stop her eyes from taking in the rest of his powerful body, at ease in the transparent water. She got up quickly, not caring that he was watching her with an intensity hotter than the water. She started to leave the bath, but his voice stopped her.

"Rea," he said, "look at me."

There was something in his voice that made her turn and face him. She wouldn't listen to him . . . could not! But she shivered, in spite of the heat of the room, and under his eyes, the water lapping about her became a living thing, a caressing hand that cupped her breasts and stroked her inner thighs. The naked want in his eyes made her sigh, suddenly. It was an acknowledgment. This time, she knew there was no going back.

"I promised myself—after the last time—that I wouldn't bother you again," Ivan was saying. "I tried not to think of you. I went with other women, trying to forget you. Nothing mattered or worked for me . . . except you. When I saw you today—"

She caught her breath raggedly. "Oh, Ivan," she said, and held out her hands helplessly. He caught one of them, kissing the palm roughly, passionately.

"I want you," he said. "You know that, of course, but you don't know how deeply. You told me that for you making love must involve some kind of commitment. I want you to understand that . . . that I'm in love with you."

The pain in her chest was unbearable . . . but as he spoke these words, the pain seemed to burst, explode away into a moment of joy so intense, it was worse than pain.

"I'm not sure what love is," he said, "but I do know that I want you as I've wanted no other woman. I want to protect you, and at the same time, sometimes I want to murder you!"

"I feel the same way about you," Rea confessed.

"I'm trying to be honest, *duschenka*. We're like the *Tanabata* bamboos we threw into the water. . . . I don't know where our feelings for each other will take us. But right now, you are everything I love and want and respect in a woman. I want to be a part of you and a part of your life. If I could bring the moon down from the sky for you, I would."

She felt her body yearn towards him as he spoke. She couldn't bear the distance between them any longer. "I don't need any moon," she whispered. Her arms went around his neck, drawing his face down to hers. They kissed slowly, unhurriedly, as if all time itself waited for them. Then their kiss deepened, became more sensuous, more urgent. Rea felt dizzy as Ivan caressed her tenderly, his hands brushing her nipples as lightly as the water itself, lingering on the upthrust, sensitive tips.

"You're so beautiful, Rea. Come here to me. . . ."

He drew her to him, setting her on his knees. She opened

to him as water does to moonlight, parched earth to rain. And now, one body and one movement of desire and fulfillment, they came together into one universe that was giddy with a rapture Rea had never dreamt could be hers. This was where she had always known she would be. This was heaven . . . and home.

- 13 -

REA AWOKE TO bright sunlight, which streamed through the open wood-and-paper screens. Moving her head on her pillow, she remembered Ivan's closeness. A slow warmth coursed through her . . . no longer the fires of raging desire, but the dreamy glow of her fulfilled body. They had come back to the room shamelessly hand in hand last night, to find the night quilts spread on the floor, the screen opened a little to show the rain-drenched garden under white stars. The summer storm had passed, and the Celestial Lovers in the sky were meeting—just as the lovers on earth had met. Rea had slipped into Ivan's arms as naturally as if she had always been there. Through the long, magical night, they had loved and talked, drowsed to wake to more loving.

Rea stretched luxuriously, remembering the feel of his muscled body against hers. How gently he had held her, and yet what a powerful lover he had been! Her cheeks flushed at the memory of each moment, each caress that had drugged her with a joy so intense she could hardly bear it even now. And the talk between them had been as good as the lovemaking. Stripped of masks or pretense, she had seen Ivan's soul . . . his warm, sensitive heart, with its instinctive courtesy, the loneliness that had been his until she came into his life. They had spoken of the past and the present . . . but not of the future. Somehow, it hadn't seemed important, because any future would be theirs to share.

It had been dawn before Rea finally fell into a deep sleep, and before she did, Ivan had kissed her and told her he would be gone when she woke. "I have to be in Tokyo this morning, so I'll be up early," he told her. "I'll get through quickly, though . . . and come back by evening. Will you wait for me at the Wynns'?"

"I'll wake up when you go . . . promise to wake me up," she had murmured, but he had let her sleep. She turned her face to kiss the hard Japanese pillow on which he had rested his head, and then saw that the cloud of sunlight in the room was glittering on something that had been left on the pillow. Raising herself on her elbow, she found a yellow chrysanthemum, and smiled, remembering that night at Matsuyashiki. Then she saw that a ring had been slipped about the stem of the flower. It was a small ring of white gold set with four small diamonds and a midnight-blue sapphire.

"How beautiful!" Rea sat up and slid the sapphire on her ring finger. It was too loose, so she tried it on her middle finger, where it fitted perfectly. "I'm so happy," she said, and she remembered the *Tanabata* bamboo and smiled, knowing that her wish had been granted. She didn't know what the future would hold . . . but they would discuss it tonight. Possibly, she would return to Reece to publish her book . . . and then return to him. Perhaps she would never go back to America. This was something that they would work out between them.

As for Catherina . . . they had spoken of her, of course, last night, between the cool quilts. With his cheek on her breast, Ivan had said that that had been an arranged thing—a business merger, really—and did not involve any deep commitment. Though he had not said so, Ivan had made it clear that their never-formalized engagement would be soon broken.

Later that morning, Rea waited for a taxi outside the gate of the inn. When she saw a dark-blue car driving towards her, she was sure it was the cab, and stepped forward . . . only to realize that the person driving the car was Catherina da Silva.

Rea stepped backwards quickly, but it was too late. Catherina had recognized her, and brought her small car to a stop. "Why . . . Rea Harley!" she exclaimed. "You and I seem to meet in the strangest spots. Were you conducting research in this place?"

Rea felt herself flush. "Of a kind," she said. "What brings you here so early?"

"Early? My dear, it's close to noon!" Catherina drawled. "I had an appointment with my hairdresser early this morning, because I need to attend an important lunch in Osaka. Unfortunately, my hairdresser lives all the way out here in Ashiya."

A taxi had now come into view. Rea tried to say goodbye, but Catherina would not let her go. "Taxi? Why, when I am here and can take you to Osaka? Nonsense!" she said. "I insist that you ride with me."

There was no way Rea could refuse without making a scene, though Catherina was the last person she wanted to see this morning. As Rea got in beside the heiress, Catherina glanced at her in a condescending way. "Did the Akiras tell you about this teahouse?" she asked. "It's a favorite of theirs. I often come here myself, for a cup of tea or some relaxation. In this day and age, most people prefer Western-style hotels, but Ivan likes this inn very much."

Was she insinuating something? Rea remained quiet, but could not prevent herself from glancing down at her hand, where she had placed Ivan's ring. Catherina's eyes followed hers.

"What an interesting ring!" Catherina said. "May I see it?"

They had stopped for a light. Reluctantly, Rea lifted her hand, and Catherina's eyes narrowed slightly. Without comment, she allowed Rea to take her hand away, and was silent for some time as she drove out of Ashiya and down the highway. After a while, Rea asked how the summer house in Matsumoto was coming. Catherina shrugged slightly.

"Oh . . . I leave the summer house to my father and Ivan," she said, coolly. "You do know that Ivan designed it, don't you? He does many things well." There was an undercurrent of tension in her smooth voice as she continued. "Perhaps he does some things too well, don't you agree?"

With an effort, Rea forced herself to smile pleasantly. "I don't know what you mean, Catherina."

"No? Well, a word of friendly warning, my dear. You are a stranger in this country, and you don't know its customs very well. In Japan, men enjoy a certain freedom and take it as their God-given right. They think nothing of sleeping with various women in whom they have no real interest."

"Really." Rea was sure that Catherina knew about her and Ivan. Was it because of some instinct, or . . .

"That ring you're wearing," Catherina said, interrupting her thoughts. "Ivan gave it to you, didn't he?" She shook her head as Rea remained silent. "Really, that man! He has no constancy at all, you know. I last saw that same ring on the finger of one of the prettiest nightclub hostesses I've ever seen. Before that, some jazz singer was wearing it . . . and before that, someone else. It seems that it's his habit to pass it from one light o' his love to another."

"Catherina, I'd appreciate it if we quit talking about this," Rea said. "What Ivan did in the past has nothing to do with me."

Catherina laughed shortly. "Past? My dear, don't you hear what I'm saying to you? These girls aren't in Ivan's *past*. They are all current flames of his . . . his harem, if you like." She lowered his voice. "There was just recently some talk about his marrying one of them. Not a *real* marriage, you understand, just a ceremony to soothe the girl. Of course, all this will stop after we are married."

Rea said nothing. In spite of herself, the poison of Catherina's words had begun to filter through her mind. It wasn't true, she thought. Ivan loved *her*. "I don't believe you," she said.

"Don't you? Rea, face it. To Ivan, you are an unimportant interlude. Look in tonight's paper if you think differently . . . Babette Lane's column!"

Rea studied the beautiful, cold, self-satisfied face, and anger spurted in her. How dare Catherina try to ruin the happiness she had held so briefly? She put her hand on the door handle. "Would you please stop the car?" she asked. "I'd like to go home on my own."

"Here?" Catherina looked surprised, but there was a satisfied gleam in her heavy-lidded eyes. "Suit yourself, of course . . . but please believe me, all my warnings have been for your good."

I'll bet! Rea thought as she got out of the car and slammed the door. She began to walk, too angry to think of where she was or where she was going. Catherina was jealous . . . that was it. She was furious because Ivan loved her, Rea. Shivering with anger, Rea stalked on, heedless of her high-heeled shoes and white cocktail dress. Catherina had lied from beginning to end. Certainly, there must have been women in Ivan's life . . . but not now! And as for Catherina marrying Ivan . . .

Suddenly, Rea stopped walking. What had Catherina meant by telling her to look in tonight's paper? The triumph in the woman's eyes made Rea uneasy. Snatches of conversation came back to her. Akira's latest . . . merger between da Silva Techmatics and Akira Industries . . . an empire stretching over Japan and across the sea. Would the Bamboo Baron willingly let his son walk away from marrying da Silva's daughter?

She shrugged the thoughts away and forced herself to calm down. When she finally reached the Wynns', it was well into the afternoon. "Where on earth have you been?" Janet asked as Rea came in. "Tucker and I came home around three this morning, and got worried when you weren't home. I almost phoned the Akiras, but decided I'd better not." She gave Rea a long look. "You weren't with—"

Rea felt defensive. "I'm a big girl now, Janet. What if I was with Ivan?"

Jan moaned. "Oh, me," she sighed. "I was afraid so."

Rea sat down beside Janet and took her friend's hand. "It's not so bad as all that, Jan! Ivan's not the way you think he is. He may give the appearance of being a real Don Juan, but he's not."

"Are you in love with him?" Janet asked bluntly.

Rea nodded. "I tried not to be, Jan. After Bill, I never wanted to fall head over heels over any man again. But Ivan is different. We love each other."

Without another word, Janet got up from the couch and began to walk away, clutching the newspaper in her hand. There was something so unhappy and furtive in her gesture that Rea frowned. "Jan . . . you know something I should know," she said. "What is it?"

Janet looked at Rea for a second, then her shoulders slumped. With a weary gesture, she ran a hand through her thick gray curls. "I suppose you'd find out anyway," she said, and dropped the newspaper into Rea's lap. "Babette Lane's column," she added gloomily.

Rea turned the newspaper over, her fingers suddenly nerveless. Babette Lane's column... Here it was! Rea forced herself to read it slowly, but her eyes moved in nervous skips.

"... At a lunch today... Royal Hotel... announcement of the merger between da Silva Techmatics and Akira Industries." Was that all? But there was more! "At the luncheon, Diego da Silva, president of da Silva Techmatics, announced the impending marriage of his daughter, Catherina, to Mr. Jun Ivan Akira. Although the announcement was informal, da Silva said, the marriage had been a dear hope of both himself and Baron Akira, now in Paris."

She let the paper slide from her lap to the floor. A dull pain twisted inside her. "I don't believe it," she whispered.

"Are you all right?" Jan was stooping over her. When Rea nodded, the older woman sighed. "I wish I could tell you it was a pack of lies, but it isn't. It's been coming for a long time."

"But... but Ivan is in Tokyo today!" Rea seized on this straw of hope. "How could they become engaged?"

"As Diego da Silva pointed out, this isn't a formal announcement. However, such an announcement has been handed to the press. Tucker got one at *Outlook* today. He told me so when I called to ask him about Babette's story."

Rea got up. She could not feel her knees or legs, but somehow they carried her across the room and to her bedroom. She sank down on her bed. Janet followed her. "I'm all right," she told Janet.

"Are you? You look as if you might faint or something. Put your head between your knees and breathe deeply."

In spite of herself, Rea laughed. Her laughter was harsh, without humor... a laugh she had heard from Ivan in the past. Ivan... she couldn't help thinking of him, even now. Damn him! she thought. He'd used her... and he'd gotten what he wanted. All those promises—all that talk about love and respect—were meant to get her into bed, and he'd accomplished that. After all, he'd had enough experience, she supposed.

"Well," she said shortly, "I guess I made a fool of myself. Good for me. I know one thing for sure, though . . . once a fool, always a fool, Janet! After this, if a man even looks at me with bedroom eyes, I'll run, not walk, away!"

Her voice broke on the last word, and Janet came to her, wrapping comforting wiry arms around her. I will not cry for you, Ivan Akira, Rea thought, but the tears were there, and spilled out of her eyes. Golden eyes, he had called them last night. Resolutely, she pushed herself free of Janet's arms.

"He's coming here tonight, Jan."

"Here!" Janet's eyes sparked fire. "I'll tell him to get lost; don't worry. You don't have to see him."

"No, I do want to see him. I have to give him back this." Rea twisted off the sapphire-and-diamond ring, held it in the palm of her hand. Painfully, she curled her fingers around the ring, hiding it in her palm. "I want to tell him . . . goodbye," she added. "It's something I need to do on my own."

Feeling brittle and hard, like spun glass, she was terrified of the moment Ivan would come through the door . . . and yet, she looked forward to it. She would hurt him, somehow . . . hurt him as he had hurt her. She would lacerate him and his pride, and drive away the memory of his voice, his smile, his taste.

When the doorbell finally rang, however, she could not answer it at once. She felt numb. It rang again before she forced herself to her feet and stumbled to the door. When she saw Ivan standing here, a wave of dizziness spread through her at the sight of his smile . . . tender and warm and loving, open to her and their night together.

"Rea," he said, and reached out to pull her to him. Even now, something in her opened to him. It cost her the world to turn her back to him.

"Have you seen the evening paper, Ivan?" she asked, not trusting herself to look at him. "Babette Lane's column."

"I don't make a practice of reading her column." Ivan sounded puzzled. "Her prose is too gushing for my taste. Why do you ask? You sound strange, Rea."

Unsteadily, she walked to the couch, where the evening paper lay. She picked it up and handed it to Ivan without a word. He read it, a frown appearing between his eyebrows as his eyes raced over the print. Then he swore softly and put the paper down.

"Rea, I had no idea . . . about the merger, yes! I told you that my father and Diego have been working on the details for a long time. But about the engagement . . . no."

"Presumably, the engagement was one of the 'details' they discussed." Rea felt the urge to burst into tears, but held herself cool and aloof. "Tucker says that a formal announcement has been handed to the press."

Ivan's frown deepened. "Catherina must have gone ahead with that . . . without discussing it with me. I'll speak with her."

"There's no need." Rea heard herself speaking as if from far away. The tumultuous pounding of her heart had changed, turned dull and slow, as if something inside her way slowly dying. "I met Catherina today after I . . . I left the Chrysanthemum inn. She told me about your engagement and . . . and about the history of the ring."

"The ring?" His voice had sharpened suddenly. "But then, if you know, you'll understand how I feel about you!"

She stared at him, unable to believe his words. How could the tender, sensitive lover of last night have just said that? How could he tell her he felt for her as he did for hostesses and bar-girls scattered throughout Osaka? Rea clenched her small hands at her sides. She was suddenly filled with impotent rage at herself, and at him. In that moment, Ivan reminded her of Bill . . . Bill, with his selfishness and charm. Ivan probably felt that all he needed to do was sweet-talk her again, murmur words of love and appreciation, and she would fall into his arms. But not this time!

He said, "I told you how Catherina and I feel about each other. If I explain matters to her, she'll understand."

Another lie. Catherina probably was madly in love with Ivan . . . hungry for him, as she, Rea, still was. Rea couldn't believe it, but when Ivan stepped towards her, a part of her still yearned for his nearness. With a sharp, decisive gesture, she thrust her hand towards him, opening her fist to reveal the ring he had given her.

"Please take this back, Ivan. I don't want it."

Bewilderment, then anger, flicked in his green eyes. "Rea," he said, "don't push me. I can explain what all this means, but don't push me. . . ."

"Don't push *you?*" Rage gusted through her voice. "What kind of man *are* you, Ivan Akira? You used me last night, just as you used the other women to whom you gave this ring."

If his face had been angry a moment ago, it was now like iron. "I advise you to be quiet," he said, his voice quiet, but so angry that she knew she'd hurt him. Well, she wanted to hurt him more . . . hurt him as she was hurting! She flung the ring at him, watched it bounce on the grass mat on the floor.

"Take it and give it to some other bar-girl or nightclub hostess," she said clearly. "Just don't come near me again."

For a moment, she thought she'd gone too far. His eyes blazed, and he clenched his fists as if he wanted to hit her. Then, without a word, he picked up the ring and turned his back on her. Striding to the door, he pulled it open and shut it behind him.

She could hear his footsteps walking swiftly away, and now the tears came. She put her hands to her mouth to stifle the sobs, but they came anyway. She had meant to tear at Ivan and hurt him . . . and she knew she had succeeded. But in doing so, she had inflicted even greater pain on herself.

- 14 -

FOR MANY LONG MINUTES, Rea stood where she was, watching the closed door. After her first few deep sobs, she found she couldn't even cry. It was as if the comfort of grieving had been denied her, and she would remember nothing more than the fury she had seen etched on Ivan's handsome face. He would never forgive her now . . . and she could never forgive or forget him.

She turned to face the empty living room, wishing that Jan were there . . . or Tucker. She needed someone to hold onto, someone to be near. Blindly, she stared around the room, and then saw that some files were stacked behind the living-room couch. For a second, she couldn't figure out what they were, and then Rea remembered Tucker's half-joking comment about photographs he'd brought her from the *Outlook* archives. Seeing them now was like an omen.

I don't need people to hang onto, Rea thought. I have my work. She repeated the words over and over, like a charm or incantation. Gradually, she became calm, so that her hands no longer shook. She would look over the files now . . . perhaps find something of value for her book. And find something of value she did, in the third file she looked through. Her attention fixed on a photograph of a blond woman in theatrical costume. Even under the blond wig of Tosca and the theatrical makeup, Rea recognized Alexandra Ivanovna.

She pulled out the photograph and studied it carefully. Was it because *Tosca* was a sad opera that Alexandra's eyes were so sad? Her mouth was sorrowful, young and vulnerable, and one hand was raised to her throat in a poignant gesture. On the hand was a small ring . . . distinct against the slender white hand.

"Oh, my God," Rea breathed.

She got to her feet and pushed the photograph under the living-room lamp, staring at the hand with the ring. It was a small ring . . . the one ring Alexandra had worn in the photo Lady Sachiko had shown her. The ring was made of four diamonds and a dark stone . . . a sapphire.

"Oh, dear God," Rea whimpered.

He had given her his mother's ring . . . probably the dearest treasure he possessed on earth . . . and she had flung it at him, with talk about bar-girls wearing the priceless heirloom. "But I didn't know," Rea told herself. "Oh, I didn't know! How could I, when Catherina . . ."

But she realized she should have known, instinctively, that Ivan could do nothing like this. She should have trusted him, and her love for him. She felt physically ill. Then common sense made her put down the photo and hurry to the phone. She would telephone Ivan . . . she would explain. With numb fingers, she dialed the phone number of the Akiras' Osaka home. She prayed that Ivan would be home, but the maid who answered told her that the master had briefly returned, then gone out for the night. No, she did not know when he would be back.

Rea let the receiver slide into place and pressed her fingers to her aching temples. Where had Ivan gone? She repressed the desire to run out the door and search for him through the city. It didn't matter that Ivan had loved her last night; she had surely killed his love now. She remembered the intensity of his anger, and felt a rush of nausea roil through her. And there was Catherina . . . Catherina, who had lied to keep Rea from the man she wanted to marry. Whatever Catherina wanted from the marriage—a merger, or power, or wealth—she was determined to have him. What chance did Rea stand? There was no way Ivan would come back to her after tonight. She had driven him straight into Catherina's arms. Surely he would marry Catherina now.

She resolved not to telephone Ivan, or to have any contact with the Akira family again. Next day, when Lady Sachiko telephoned, she begged Janet to take the call, to thank the elderly lady for her kindness on *Tanabata* night. Janet reported that Lady Sachiko had enquired after Rea's health, and had given the news that Ivan was in Hong Kong on company business and would be gone for several days. Midori had broken off her *omiyai* with Hideo and seemed much happier.

"Thanks," Rea told her friend. "Thanks for running interference for me. I . . . I don't think I want to get involved with the family any more, though I'm fond of Lady Sachiko and Midori. They'll probably be busy, anyway, preparing for the—the wedding."

She plunged back into her work. Tucker was particularly helpful . . . and so, surprisingly enough, was Professor Inariyama.

The professor took quite an interest in Rea. She often went to seminars he conducted for professors throughout the country, and frequently they had tea together and discussed the problems of modern education. Rea felt totally at ease with him, and even told Janet that she wished she had another month . . . just so that she could learn more from Inariyama.

"I'd like to teach here in this country, but that's not possible," she said with a sigh. "Their teachers' union would never let a foreigner in. Still, wouldn't it be wonderful? Once, the great Nando said I had a 'Japanese heart.' I have a feeling he was right."

Janet was noncommittal in her reply, but her face showed concern. The Wynns were convinced that Rea was working herself to the bone, and indeed, she had lost weight in the last few weeks. Tucker and Janet were constantly after her to go out with them, tempting her with a concert, the Kabuki, a performance of Shakespeare's *Hamlet* in Japanese. Occasionally, Rea weakened and went with them . . . just as she weakened when Tucker announced his intention to take Janet and Rea to the *Tenjin Matsuri*.

"You can't go back to America without seeing the biggest festival in Osaka," he said, one evening over supper.

"It started today, didn't it?" Janet asked, picking up Tucker's lead immediately. "When I was coming back from the clinic, I ran into a procession . . . girls and boys all dressed up in old-fashioned costumes, carrying a palanquin of flowers. I understand there are going to be lighted boats, and music and fireworks, all along the Dojima River tomorrow."

They both looked at Rea, who held up her hands in surrender. "All right, I give up!"

Tucker looked delighted as he explained that he had three press tickets for the following night. This meant that they would be able to occupy the press box, right on the Dojima River where the lighted boats would pass. "Good thing, too. You wouldn't see a thing, otherwise, because I have a hunch all Osaka will be there!"

The following evening, it seemed he was right. Rea looked at the crowds of people that lined the street en route to the river, and wondered how everyone could look so cheerful and happy even while they were being squashed one against the other. To entertain the crowds were bands, parades of costumed youths and girls, the boys holding aloft old-time palanquins decked with Japanese lanterns and flowers. As Rea and the Wynns battled their way to the press box, a small child in a bright kimono with a flower in her hair looked up at Rea and smiled shyly. Rea smiled back, her eyes suddenly smarting as she remembered the Kimura children in the hospital long ago.

"This way!" Tucker was perspiring as he practically hauled Rea and Janet the last few yards to the press box. Fortunately, the wooden stand was built several feet higher than the ground, so that it commanded a view of the Dojima River. Some way upstream, many boats were being readied to sail downstream, together with their complement of lanterns, music and drums.

"Quite a sight, aren't they?"

Rea cringed as she heard Babette Lane's nasal voice at her shoulder. She should have realized Babette would be here tonight! The reporter's hair was piled even higher than usual on her head; her heavily made-up eyes were snapping with curiosity.

"Well, Rea Harley!" Babette said. "I'm surprised to see you here." She nodded at another box some distance from theirs. "I thought you'd be with the bigwigs over there. That's the Akiras' special viewing box . . . or didn't you know?"

With an effort, Rea let her eyes roam coolly in the direction of Babette's nod. She made out Lady Sachiko and Midori . . . and Catherina. Ivan was not there. With a thankful sigh, Rea turned back to the columnist. "Why should I be invited to share the Akiras' box?" she asked. "Any business dealings we've had are over."

"Really?" Babette cocked her head like a slightly malicious parakeet. "I must tell you, my dear, that at one time I suspected that you and Ivan . . . well, it was so obvious that you were attracted to each other! Between you and me, I think Catherina was getting jealous. Not that I think she cares for the man . . . but there was all that business about the merger, you know."

"She had no cause for jealousy," Rea said stiffly. Janet's eyes darted daggers at Babette.

"Of course not! I suppose that's why Ivan Akira's headed towards the press box now?" Babbette cooed. Her eyes took in Rea's telltale blush. "Perhaps he's just coming to discuss the details of his wedding, with the press. I understand they're getting married in November."

Rea turned away from the mocking words. She could see Ivan clearly, because of his height . . . and very certainly, he was walking towards the press box. As if something had passed between them in spite of the distance, Ivan looked up . . . and their eyes locked. Rea saw the surprise in his green eyes . . . and the sudden cold bitterness as he realized that she was there.

She couldn't see him here . . . not now. . . . Nor could she ignore him. Murmuring to Janet that she'd forgotton something in the car, she slipped out of the press box and began to push her way back the way she had come. She walked blindly, thrusting her way through the crowds. A voice shouted, "Here come the boats!" and people thronged about her, nearly knocking her down. Resolutely, Rea kept moving away from the river; but the crowd surged forward bearing Rea with it. There was no way she could withstand the movement of thousands of determined bodies. She caught her breath in a gasp as her foot slipped . . . and she half fell, before being caught by the eddy of bodies. Panic filled her. Rea opened her mouth in a soundless cry as she found herself being lifted off her feet and carried helplessly forward. Five yards forward . . . she had lost her shoe! . . . ten yards . . . and now, her leg slipped under her. She was falling. . . .

She stopped falling, caught this time not by the crowd around her but by someone standing behind her. Gratefully, she turned to the person, who was still holding her, steadying her while the people surged around them. "Thank you—" she began, then stopped as she looked into Ivan's cold green eyes.

"You were stupid to leave the press box," were his first words to her. Gone was the smooth mask of mockery . . . and any sign of warmth. "You could have been trampled, the way you were going against the crowd!"

"How—how did you get here!"

His lip twisted. "I saw you leave the box, and knew you'd be hurt. It seemed that someone had to go after you . . . so I did."

She could not face him. "I tried to reach you . . . that evening," she stammered. "I was wrong about the ring. Wrong about the things I said to you."

"It doesn't matter. You believed what people told you, Rea . . . not your heart. Or maybe you did believe your heart. It isn't important now."

Bleakly, she knew that he was right. "I hear you are getting married in November."

He nodded curtly. "Yes. I imagine you will have left Japan by then." He was still holding her, and even with people all around them, jostling and pushing, she felt the slow, inexorable fire build up within her. Wouldn't it ever end? she wondered. Would she never be rid of his hold on her, that ability he had to make her feel vulnerable and unbalanced and hungry for him?

"Yes, I leave next month."

"A pity. I would have sent you an invitation to the wedding." The cruelty of his words hit her like a slap in the face. She winced. Without another word, he began to lead her back towards the press box. Limping, with one shoe on, Rea felt humiliated, deeply hurt. Why did he have to say that? She did not look at him again as he brought her to the edge of the box and then let her go.

"Goodbye," he said, and then bowed to her gracefully

in spite of the crowd. She forced herself to meet his eyes, to show him it did not matter to her what he said or did, and saw a look in those clear green eyes that filled her with confusion before he turned away. It was not hate she saw in Ivan's eyes. It was . . . what? Pain? longing? Something in her reached blindly for him.

"Ivan . . ." she called, but her voice was drowned suddenly as the heavens exploded. Fireworks splashed high into the sky over the ships floating down the river. Lights on the water reflected thunderous sounds and whistling lights, and Rea's eyes turned, involuntarily, to the sky.

When she looked down again, a second later, Ivan had gone.

- 15 -

REA WORKED RELENTLESSLY through the burning end-of-July days and the first week of August. The days of the Japanese summer were hotter than anything she had experienced in Boston, even in the dog days, and she began to work during the nights . . . because it was cooler, she told the Wynns. Janet said nothing, though her worry showed clearly in her eyes. She seemed to know that Rea was afraid to sleep too much; her dreams were about Ivan, and disturbed her more than she could bear.

Feeling the way she did, Rea was glad when the second week of August brought news that the Akira family had gone to Matsumoto to spend the important religious holiday of *Obon* at the da Silvas' new summer house. With Ivan out of Osaka, perhaps she could put him out of her mind.

It didn't work that way. Babette Lane's column gave an account of the Akiras' doings every single day. Rea stopped reading the column, and it was Jan Wynn who gave her the news of Midori's illness.

"Apparently, she hasn't felt well for some time, and she really took sick in Matsumoto," she told Rea one morning over breakfast. "They've brought her back to Osaka, or so Babette writes."

Rea crumbled a slice of toast absently on her plate. "Do you think I should phone and see how she is?" Janet's shrewd glance made her flush. "They *were* very kind to me, Jan . . . Midori and Lady Sachiko."

"I don't think it would be wise," Janet said flatly. "You're leaving in ten days, Rea. You have plenty of loose ends to tie up . . . and some more work to do. Midori will have the finest doctors, believe me." As Rea still hesitated, Janet added, "If you like, I'll try to find out how she's doing. Doctors always like to talk shop, and I can probably discover who's treating Midori."

Rea agreed that Janet's advice was sensible, and when she learned that Midori was suffering from nothing worse than bronchitis, tried to put the Akiras out of her mind. Janet was right... there was a lot of work left to do, and she had many loose ends to tie up, including saying goodbye to Professor Inariyama.

Rea hated to do this. She had become very close to the Japanese educator in the past few months. She phoned Inariyama's house, and was invited to lunch with the professor and his wife.

She took along a small gift for the occasion, and presented it after lunch. He took it with a small, preoccupied frown. "Rea-san," he began, "I am most distressed that you are leaving us. You have been a great help to me. I am going to ask a favor of you."

"I am honored," Rea said politely, expecting him to ask her for some materials from America. She was stunned when he said nothing of the kind. Instead, he told her that he had decided he wanted to start a small private school of his own.

"You know that my ideas on education are different from my colleagues'," he told her. "I believe that a new, progressive way of thinking could do great things for our country. The school would be a high school, and it would be very small, at first. But I—and the professors who would start with me—would be free to teach our own way!"

He paused, and gave her a long look. "I would like you to be on the staff with me, Rea-san."

Rea was stunned. It had been a dream of hers, as she'd told Janet a long time ago, to stay here in Japan and teach. And to teach under Inariyama.... She wanted to tell him this, but she couldn't find the words, and he misinterpreted her silence.

"I realize that it would seem a step down," he said hastily. "You are a professor in a university... this would only be a high school. But think of it! You could teach language and comparative history... you could mold the minds of intelligent young people..." He leaned forward eagerly.

"I don't want you to decide right away, Rea-san. Please think about it! Together, we could lay the foundations for a new movement in education."

Finally, she could speak. "I can't believe you're offering this chance to me," she said, huskily. He held up a hand.

"Not another word! I want you to think very carefully. You would have to stay in Japan . . . it would be years before you could return to your country—if, indeed, you ever could! There would be problems with immigration, and we would need to discuss salary. I will be sending you a formal letter soon, and when that arrives, please give me an answer. Until then, ponder what I have said to you, Rea-san." In spite of himself, he leaned forward again. "I really hope," he said, "you decide to stay!"

Rea left the Inariyama home with a smile that seemed to cover her whole face. To be offered a position by Inariyama! To be able to stay here! It was better than anything she had ever hoped or dreamed. Her mind filled with plans, the formation of her own curriculum. The long years of worry and insecurity seemed to float away from her, leaving her serene, relaxed, confident. "Wait till the Wynns hear," she exulted. "Will we ever celebrate!"

When the bus reached her stop, Rea practically skipped off. She was humming a Japanese folksong when she came in view of the Wynn's apartment. Then the song died in her throat. A familiar white Lancia was sitting in the parking lot, and Ivan was waiting for her. She stared as he strode towards her.

"Where have you been?" he demanded. "I've been waiting for you for an hour. I tried to telephone you, but no one was home." She started to speak, but he cut her off. "Pack a few things. I'm driving you to Kyoto."

She pulled herself together. "Kyoto! I'm not going to Kyoto or anywhere else with you." She tried to walk past him, but he grasped her by the arm, his strong grip painful in its intensity.

"It's not me who's asking you, Rea. Midori is ill, and has been asking for you. We didn't want to bother you, Aunt Sachi and I, but she's not getting any better."

His voice was bleak, and Rea swung around to face him.

"Midori asking for me? But . . . I thought she only had bronchitis! Is she seriously ill?"

He shook his head. "We don't know. The doctors aren't sure what she has. She's been checked out by the best specialists. They can't find a thing wrong with her, but she keeps on dropping weight and has lost all her old spirit. She doesn't even argue with me any more."

Rea bit her lip. Ivan was trying to joke, but there was real fear in his voice. She remembered the impish girl who had welcomed her in such a friendly way, and made up her mind. "It'll just take me a few minutes to pack some things," she said. "I'll write a note telling the Wynns where I am."

He nodded gratefully. "You know I wouldn't have asked you if it wasn't for Midori," he said. She was hurrying away, but his grip still held her. "You needn't worry about . . . anything," he told her, and Rea felt the clear green eyes look at her and then away. "I give you my word that I won't . . . bother you. That's all over."

Rea couldn't speak. A lump of pain had risen in her throat, and she could only nod as Ivan finally released his hold and she could go into the apartment building, away from him.

They were silent on their drive to Kyoto. Ivan made no attempt at conversation, and Rea did not want to initiate any talk. Once they entered Kyoto proper, however, Ivan glanced at her.

"I went to the Daisen temple the other morning," he said quietly. "I watched the sun come up. I thought it would be changed, somehow, but it wasn't. I thought of you."

What was he trying to tell her? Was he trying to say that he still cared for her? That some things never changed? "Tell me about Midori," she said. "Are you sure she's not sick because you're trying to foist Hideo on her?"

Ivan frowned at her, then laughed without humor. "You've got your facts wrong, Professor Rea Harley. That business with Hideo is long over. We gave it up before we went to Matsumoto. I understand that Hideo is doing *omiyai* with another young woman now. Whatever ails Midori, it's not Hideo."

"Was she very sick—with the bronchitis, I mean?"

Ivan turned his car through the gravel pathway. "She was hospitalized for some time. Aunt and I did what we could, and Catherina nursed Midori devotedly. Yet, she only got worse."

The tall gates of Matsuyashiki rose before them. Rea felt as though memories were pressing upon her. To rid herself of the sudden sadness she felt, she said, "Does she know I'm coming?"

"No. I wasn't sure you'd want to come, and didn't want to get her hopes up." Ivan sounded his car horn, and the Matsuyashiki gates were instantly opened by Jiiya, the gardener. As Rea got out of the car, Lady Sachiko came hurrying to her and clasped her by both hands.

"Rea-san!" Lady Sachiko's narrow eyes were glistening with happy tears. "I am so glad you are here. Midori has been wanting to see you. She's in the garden."

"I'll go to her right now." Rea said. She found Midori sitting beside the pool in a low rattan chair. She was dressed in a cotton summer *yukata,* and though her hair had been combed neatly, there was an unkempt air about her. She looked, Rea thought, rather like a flower drooping for lack of water.

Then Midori looked up and saw Rea. A flash of pleasure lit up the young girl's eyes, and she held out her arms. Rea gave her a warm hug, and was shocked to realize how much weight Midori had lost. "Hello, Midori-chan," she said, using the affectionate and familiar "chan." "I've missed you. Ivan tells me you've been ill."

Midori's face, flushed for a moment, now became pale again. "I don't feel sick," she said in a listless voice.

Rea sat in a chair next to Midori and took the younger girl's hand in hers. "Does it hurt you anywhere?" she asked anxiously. Something definitely was wrong. No wonder Ivan was so worried! "Please tell me, Midori-chan," she went on gently.

"Inside," Midori whispered, and tears spurted into her eyes. She turned her head like a child and rubbed her sleeve across her eyes. "It hurts inside, Rea. Only you would understand. It's Hideo."

Rea was shocked. "But I heard the *omiyai* with Hideo had been broken off!"

The tears poured down Midori's frail cheeks. "That's just it, Rea . . . I treated him abominably, and he went away. He wants nothing more to do with me. It wasn't till too late that I realized . . . realized . . ."

"That you loved him!" Rea smiled a little sadly. How young Midori was, she thought. She felt old, herself, and suddenly tired. "But what's so awful about that? Call him, and tell him—"

"No!" The word exploded out of Midori, and she grabbed Rea by the shoulders, holding her tightly. "That's one thing I mustn't do. Hideo wouldn't want me any more. I made him lose face. Ca-Catherina says he's in love with some other girl, anyway." She turned away her head and wept. "He never wants to see me again!"

Rea frowned. "I don't believe it. Hideo really loved you. Supposing Lady Sachiko or Ivan talked with him?"

Midori shok her head fiercely. "Promise me you won't say a word to either of them. I've disgraced them enough. I mustn't shame the family further. I was spoiled . . . wilful. I acted like a ch-child, and sent away the only man I could love. It serves me right if I die!"

Rea didn't comment, but tried to comfort Midori. Love was never easy, she thought. Or rather, *love* was easy. It was the rest of it . . . pride . . . "face" . . . commitment. Those were the hard things! "Midori, now that I'm here, you have got to get better," Rea finally said.

"I'll try." The ghost of a smile lit Midori's face. "I can talk to you as though you're my own sister. I know you can understand me, because of what you feel for my brother." Rea looked at her in surprise, and Midori laughed sadly. "Forgive me? I couldn't help noticing how you felt about each other."

"If there was anything, it's over now. He's going to marry Catherina."

Midori nodded with a sigh. "Yes," she said without enthusiasm. "Catherina. I hope he will be happy with her . . . but she is a cold woman, Rea. I—I can't say I'll be glad to have her for a sister-in-law."

They were interrupted by Lady Sachiko and Ivan's coming into the garden. Behind them were two maids. One carried a small folding table, the other a tea tray. Jiiya now arrived, with more rattan chairs. Midori made a face at Rea.

"They are trying to fatten me up, Rea."

Rea decided it was time to be firm. "You have worried them very much, Midori-chan. You talked about shaming them and so on... well, I'm going to give you some advice as a friend. You must get well and strong, if only for their sake. When people love you as Ivan and your aunt do, it puts a responsibility on you. Eventually, there'll be another man you love..."

"Will there ever be another man for you besides Ivan?" Midori challenged.

Rea lifted her chin. "Yes," she said, and remembered Inariyama, the school, her book. She clung to these things for a moment, and felt calm enough to add, "Now, sit up and eat a little, like a good girl. I am your doctor now, and my patients all have to do as I say!"

Midori gave a ghost of her old giggle, and when the tea things were set up, said casually, "I think I feel like eating a cake today, Aunt Sachi."

Aunt Sachiko beamed at her niece, and the look she gave Rea was one of pure gratitude. Ivan drew Rea aside as the old lady filled the tea cups.

"Thank you," he said simply, and warmly.

His words made her blink back sudden tears. She looked at the tender scene of aunt and niece and felt a sudden emptiness, as if she had been invited to watch a feast in which she couldn't share. Then, mentally, she shook herself. She had more important things to consider now.

"Ivan, tell me... you mentioned before that Hideo was engaged in seeing another young lady. Does that mean he no longer cares for Midori?"

"Not at all." Ivan sighed. "He worships the ground she walks on. But she made it so plain she hated him, that all of us decided he shouldn't press the matter further." He gave her a curious look. "Why do you ask?"

How to get those two together? She had promised not to tell Ivan or Lady Sachiko. But... she hadn't promised not to tell Hideo! Rea suddenly felt like smiling. It really was very simple, after all!

"I wanted to know about Hideo because I need to ask him a question for my book," she said glibly. "I had been planning to call him today, before you arrived and brought me here to Kyoto."

"Do it from here," Ivan said...just as Rea hoped he would. She pretended to think it over, then nodded.

"Would that be all right? Only, don't tell Midori. I don't want her to be upset, thinking of Hideo"—which was true enough!

Ivan led her to a phone inside Matsuyashiki and dialed the number for her. For a moment, Rea was afraid that he was going to stand there and listen to her conversation with Hideo, but when the phone rang in Hideo's house, he nodded and left her. Unfortunately, it was Hideo's mother who answered. She said that he was not at home.

"Is there some message I might give him?" she asked. Rea racked her brain. She could not blurt out the whole story to Hideo's mother... but she might not have a chance to call again without Midori's knowing.

"Please tell him that Rea Harley is at Matsuyashiki and would like to speak with him," she said. "I've been asked down because Midori-san isn't feeling well, and I thought it would be good time to ask Hideo-san about something for my book."

Now, if Hideo's mother only repeated that message word for word, Hideo was sure to call! Rea only hoped that he wouldn't telephone while Midori was around.

By the time Rea rejoined the others, shadows were beginning to sweep across the garden. A small breeze had sprung up, cooling the air of summer heat for a little while. Ivan carried Midori to her room, and Lady Sachiko went indoors to supervise supper. Rea stayed where she was in the chrysanthemum garden, listening for the ring of the phone. She wished Hideo would hurry and telephone.

"Well, good evening! This is a pleasant surprise!"

Rea started at the sound of Catherina's familiar drawl. Looking up from where she sat, she noted that Catherina did not look too pleased to see her. Wearing simple white slacks and a stunning blouse, the heiress gave Rea a decidedly unfriendly glance before sitting down in one of the rattan chairs. *Why are you here?* the look plainly asked.

Rea explained that Ivan had asked her to visit Midori. "Oh... Midori!" With a wave of her hand, Catherina dismissed Midori. "That silly young girl." Rea felt her dislike for Catherina grow as she remembered the last time she had spoken with her. Apparently, Catherina remembered it too.

"I understand you returned the ring to Ivan," she said calmly. "It was the wisest thing you could do. Like should marry like, you know. Ivan and I have the same goals . . . and we come from a similar background. It will be a successful match."

Rea looked at the haughty, beautiful face and felt a shiver run through her. Oh, Ivan, my darling, she thought sadly. Midori was right . . . Catherina was a very cold woman. She talked about marriage as if it were a business deal. "I wish you happiness," Rea said, finally. "I truly do." For Ivan's sake, her mind added.

Before Catherina could reply, Lady Sachiko came to call Rea in to dinner. She seemed surprised to see Catherina. "I didn't know you were in Kyoto, Catherina-san," she said. "Please stay and have supper with us. Midori is much better, thanks to Rea-san."

Catherina's eyebrows rose as Lady Sachiko gave Rea a gentle little pat of approval. "Have you been taking lessons in medicine from Dr. Wynn?" she asked Rea. Her half-hidden sarcasm made Rea wince. She remained silent, but Ivan spoke from behind Lady Sachiko.

"Rea is no ordinary medical doctor," he said, making everyone turn towards him. He had come so softly, they had not heard him approach. "She has a rare quality, though, and that is caring. Midori is better because Rea honestly wants her to get well. My aunt and I are grateful for 'Dr.' Rea."

He spoke with such warmth that Rea felt her cheeks flame. The happiness she felt at that moment was something no one could take away from her. Catherina bit her lip but rallied at once.

"Well, then . . . let us join the good doctor for dinner and see how the patient is," she said laughing.

All during the meal, Catherina talked about the November wedding, the honeymoon in Geneva and Paris, her gown. Ivan only seldom joined her monologue, and Lady Sachiko made polite replies. Midori remained quiet, and only ate when Rea nudged her or coaxed her to do so.

Rea herself found she had no appetite in spite of the fact that the Kobe steak in front of her was excellent, the vegetables fresh and delicately cooked, the mousse with custard sauce delicious. Lady Sachiko was about to ring for coffee, when a sudden commotion broke out.

"What on earth! . . ." Catherina exclaimed, as a loud pounding noise began. Ivan got to his feet.

"It sounds as if someone is trying to break the gate down," he said. He looked at his aunt. "Are we expecting anyone?"

Lady Sachiko shook her head, but before she could speak, a hoarse voice yelled, "Let me in! Let me in immediately, I tell you!"

Midori turned red, then pale as death. "Hideo!" she gasped.

Lady Sachiko looked aghast. "Oh, my heavens!" she groaned. "What shall we do? He must be drunk. Midori, go to your room. Ivan, please do something!"

As she spoke, they heard the gate opening, the roaring of a car motor, and then a car door slamming. Moments later, Hideo came racing into the house. He was wild-eyed, his glasses askew on his nose, and he did not look like the mild, humorous young man Rea knew. Ivan tried to stop him at the door.

"Hideo, what's the meaning of all this?" he demanded.

Hideo pushed Ivan aside and stormed into the room. He saw Rea first. "Midori! What's wrong with . . ." His eyes then focused on the young woman, who gave a sudden cry and bolted out of the room. Shouting her name, Hideo ran after her. Ivan started in pursuit of Hideo.

"Hideo, come back! She doesn't want to see you. . . ."

"Ivan, you're wrong! She does!"

Ivan stopped where he was, and turned to face Rea, a deep frown between his eyebrows. Catherina and Lady Sachiko, too, stared at her, while the servants, who had gathered in the hallway, nodded among themselves. "Explain, Rea!" Ivan said curtly.

Rea took a deep breath. She explained Midori's problem, adding that though she had promised not to speak of Hideo to Ivan or Lady Sachiko, she hadn't been bound by the same promise as far as Hideo was concerned.

"I meant to talk to him on the phone... but he wasn't in when I called. I suppose he was alarmed at the message I gave his mother," she said.

"Well, really!" Lady Sachiko gasped.

Catherina's cutting voice broke the silence. "What a stupid, thoughtless thing to do! Don't you know that the shock of seeing Hideo could cause Midori harm in her weakened condition?"

"Rea meant it for the best." Ivan's championship was so unexpected that even Catherina fell silent. "Even so, it could be that you're right, Catherina. I suppose I'd better go out there and reason with Hideo. Coming, Aunt Sachi?"

"What a terrible mess," the elderly lady moaned. Together, she and Ivan left the room, and Catherina turned on Rea.

"I suppose you feel you've been clever?" she demanded.

Rea was not feeling clever at all. It had seemed so simple when she'd thought it all out, but now... "I did it for Midori," she said, steeling herself against the look of utter dislike and contempt in Catherina's eyes.

"You shouldn't meddle where you're not wanted," Catherina said angrily. "I'm not just talking about Midori and Hideo, but also about Ivan. Believe me, you will never have his love."

She whirled and walked away from the dining room, towards the suddenly quiet garden. Rea stayed where she was until an exclamation of astonishment from Catherina made her hurry to the screen door that overlooked the garden. There, on a rattan chair beside the pool, sat Midori, her hands on her lap and her head bent, like a modest Japanese maiden. Beside her, kneeling on the sand, was Hideo. Ivan and Lady Sachiko were standing some distance away, watching calmly.

"They're together again!" Rea whispered.

Without a word, Catherina left her side and walked into the garden towards Ivan. With a glance at Rea, she threaded her arm through his in a proprietary way. Rea felt her happiness ebb away. She had united Midori and her Hideo, but her own love was as far away from her as the moon. And, in spite of her brave words to Midori earlier in the day, she knew that she could never forget him.

She turned her back on the happy couple and the others and went into the house. She asked a maid where her room was, and was led to the Chrysanthemum Room. Here, she sat quietly, not turning on the lights or going into the garden, but watching a nearly-full moon swing into the night sky. She tried not to think of Ivan and Catherina, but the thoughts came anyway.

"She won't give him what he needs," she thought. Ivan was sensitive and warm... and Catherina was cold. He would end up miserable... or else he would turn hard and cold like her. She thought of the long night they had shared at the inn, and how they had talked softly between love-making. Now, no one would bother to reach into Ivan's heart, for Rea instinctively knew Catherina would not want to.

"Goodness, Rea-san, why are you sitting here in the dark?" Lady Sachiko's brisk voice, and the light she switched on, interrupted Rea's thoughts. "Why didn't you join us in the garden?"

"I thought the family would want to be alone," Rea said. "Is Midori...?"

The old lady sank down beside Rea with a heavy sigh of satisfaction. "That bad girl," she said affectionately, "is sitting and holding Hideo's hand. They are acting like foolish children. Hideo has telephoned his parents, and Ivan will have to set up a formal meeting where the marriage can be arranged."

Rea clapped her hands. "It did work out well, then! I was so afraid, Lady Sachiko."

The old woman held up a hand. "From now, you must call me 'Aunt Sachi' like the children, for are you not a part of this family?" she demanded. Rea felt her eyes prickle with tears at her tender tone.

"I... I wonder if I shouldn't return to Osaka tonight," she said. "Now that Midori is well, there seems no point in my staying." Lady Sachiko was shocked at this proposal.

"What a scandalous idea! To think that a young woman of good family should rush back to Osaka without a proper rest! No, indeed, I shan't hear another word, Rea-san. You are exhausted. You will sleep well after a nice, hot bath, and tomorrow I am sure Midori will talk your ears off."

Rea had to admit she was ready to drop, and quickly prepared for bed. How long she slept, she didn't know, but when she awoke, it was to find moonlight flooding her room. The screen door that faced the garden was half open, and she could hear the soft rustling of a night wind. For a moment, she lay between sleep and wakefulness, then realized she wasn't alone. Ivan was sitting some distance from her sleeping quilt, watching her.

It seemed natural that Ivan should be there, as he had been in all her dreams. "Ivan?" she murmured, but he didn't come close to draw her into his arms.

"I didn't mean to wake you," he said quietly. "I just wanted to watch you while you slept. Forgive me, Rea. I'll be going now."

There was an ache of hunger in his voice, a raw tenderness that burned through the distance separating them. She sat up, her eyes on his face. In the moonlight, he seemed somehow different . . . large and powerful, but with an underlying vulnerability that matched her own. She whispered, "Ivan, you can't know how much I regretted what happened with the ring. I . . . I was terribly wrong. Will you forgive me?"

"If you will forgive the times I hurt you," he replied. He didn't move, and Rea instinctively knew that he had come to say goodbye. "We tried to hurt each other from the first . . . do you remember? I couldn't let you leave Matsuyashiki without telling you that I, too, am sorry. I want you to be happy, Rea."

He moved, as if to stand and go. She couldn't bear it. She didn't care about Catherina or about what happened tomorrow any more. She only knew she couldn't bear to have him go. "I love you," she whispered. "I love you so much." Still he didn't make a move towards her. With a little sob, she flung the quilts from her and held out her arms to him. "Oh, Ivan, hold me. Tell me you care for me, too. . . ."

He reached for her, crushing her against him. She lay half dazed against him as he kissed her hair, her eyes, her mouth. "I have been tormented, thinking of you," he groaned. "Night and day, I wanted you. I couldn't sleep or work or think for love of you. I told myself that, things being as they were, I should leave you alone. But I could not stand to be away from you tonight. I needed to see you once more. . . ."

She pressed her face against his chest and felt the warm sweetness of his skin against her lips. There was no use trying to reason with herself that she shouldn't be with Ivan . . . no use at all. The two of them were bound together, somehow. She wanted to be a part of him tonight, not just to make love but to become a part of his body and his heart and spirit. She knew that the same thoughts filled his mind, and so was surprised when he said, quite seriously, "Rea, we must talk. I have been thinking things over. All my life, I've been the son of the family . . . never questioning my father. But I can't follow my father's wishes and marry Catherina . . . not when I feel the way I do about you."

Rea's heart leaped. Was he saying what she hoped he was?

"It's not so simple, Rea," he said, reading her mind, as he always seemed to do. "You see, my father depends on me . . . and so do all the employees of Akira Industries. Somehow, I must end my marriage plans with Catherina without stopping the merger with da Silva Techmatics." There was steely determination in his green eyes. "But I will do it . . . if you are willing to be my wife."

She pressed her head back against his heart and wondered whether she was laughing or crying. "Ivan, you know that I would do anything for you." She raised her face, and he bent and kissed her, his mouth warm on hers, a promise of love and passion and tenderness. "I love you so much," she whispered.

He kissed her again. There seemed a difference in this kiss. It went beyond the mere physical for Rea. It was a pledge. "I'm happy," Ivan said quietly. "Rea, for the first time in my life, I think, I'm really happy. . . ."

He untied her *yukata,* and then his. "I adore you," he said. "My dear little one . . . I will never let you go again."

- 16 -

REA LAY WITH her head pillowed on Ivan's arm. She had awakened with the dawn and had stayed dreamily awake, too happy to fall back asleep. Ivan moved against her, pulling her to him even in sleep. She knew she could not be closer to him than she was now. She kissed the sleeping mouth, gentle and sensitive now that there was no need for masks or defenses between them. They had talked deep into the night after their first, passionate lovemaking . . . and she had told him about Inariyama's offer to her. She had been a little hesitant, afraid that he might not approve of her going ahead with a career, but he had been genuinely glad for her. It was as if, being sure of their love, he gladly accepted her work as part of her.

"I adore you, Ivan," she murmured.

His eyes flickered open, and he smiled sleepily at her, raising both arms to lock them around her and draw her close to him. "Good morning, beautiful one. I was afraid I'd dreamed you in the night, as I so often have. I thought you might be gone when I awoke."

"No such luck." She felt easy with him, relaxed and teasing. She nibbled his lips with quick kisses. "No matter what, you aren't going to get rid of me."

"I don't intend to try very hard," he said. "I'd rather keep you around. After we're married, we'll have several children. A boy to please the ancestors first . . ."

"Why, you male chauvinist! Supposing it's a girl?"

"The ancestors will be displeased," Ivan said solemnly. "I will be forced to beat you soundly . . . like this." He caressed her gently, fanning the fire of desire within her to an almost unbearable peak of pleasure. "Oh, my love . . . we'll live together for sixty years, and when we die, we'll die on the same day and be buried in the same grave. I couldn't bear to be away from you even after death."

"You're a romantic," she teased, but her eyes sparkled with ecstasy.

"Only when I'm in love," he assured her, and they began to laugh softly, muffling their laughter against each other. "I have to leave soon, Rea. They mustn't find me in your room . . . yet."

Rea smiled, thinking of the time they would openly share each others bed.

"I've got to figure out the best way of breaking the news to the family that I'm not marrying Catherina. My father is scheduled to return from Paris in a week or so. He will have to listen to me then."

His lips tightened, and Rea felt sudden fear. Suppose the baron refused to let Ivan marry her? Then the fear went away. Ivan was hers, and she his. He kissed her, a sudden, rough kiss that told her he had again read her thoughts.

"I won't let you get away from me again, my chrysanthemum flower. He will have to give in. . . . I am his only son, and he relies heavily on me. He will end up doing what I ask."

He sat up, broad chest and back muscles rippling and reached for his *yukata*. She pressed her breasts against his back, running her hands over his chest and the soft mat of dark hair and down his flat, tight belly. "You magnificent man," she murmured, letting her hand stray further. "I wonder if a Japanese woman would dare say such things to her lord and master?"

"I'd like to see the day when I'm your lord and master!" He turned and pulled her into his arms, so that she sat astride his lap. She felt his desire, the melting sweetness of her want for him. "I have to go," he murmured huskily, "but . . . not yet."

When Ivan left, the sky had begun to turn blue. Rea dozed, then woke to stretch like a contented kitten in her quilts. She felt glowingly alive. When she was married to Ivan, she thought, they could stay like this and make love all day. No one would force them apart again. . . .

"Good morning!" Midori's voice at the screen made Rea

sit up in surprise. Midori up? What time was it? She called an answer, and the screen door slid open to reveal Midori's smiling face.

"I got so hungry, I couldn't stay in bed," she said. "It is only nine o'clock, but I am going to breakfast! What do you think of that?"

"I think I'm a good doctor." Rea laughed, and Midori's glowing face sobered.

"I'll never be able to thank you for what you did for me. Hideo and I are going to be married. The family is making a big fuss about the marriage arrangements, of course! Hideo wanted us to elope, but I am a proper Japanese maiden now, and besides, my father would have been furious!"

Rea chuckled. "Midori-chan, I'm so happy for you!"

"I have never felt more joyful in my life. I only wish that you could find the same happiness with my brother." Midori glanced at Rea, then away. "He does love you, you know."

Rea wished she could tell Midori their plans, but didn't dare. Ivan had asked her to wait until he could tell his father about his decision to break with Catherina. But something made her ask, "What about Catherina?"

Midori made a face. "They never really liked each other . . . and you know what she's like. I don't think she could love anyone but herself," she said.

The household was all a-bustle when Rea and Midori made their way to the dining room. Rea noted the extra warmth the maids put into their voices as they greeted her. Lady Sachiko's good-morning hug was warm and affectionate.

"I see you brought the 'patient' to breakfast," she teased.

"I brought Rea!" Midori corrected her gaily. "Oh, wonderful! miso soup and rice and . . . can't I have some more fish?" Midori fairly rubbed her hands as she plunged into the meal.

Rea found that she, too, was starved. "You seem to like Japanese cooking," Lady Sachiko commented at last.

"I love everything about Japan." Lady Sachiko gave her a sudden sharp look, and hurriedly, Rea told about her offer from Professor Inariyama. "I am going to accept it. I hope I will live up to his high opinion of me," she added.

"My dear, how wonderful!" The elderly lady looked as eager as a young girl. "We will have you with us in Japan for longer than we'd hoped. Don't concern yourself too much about immigration . . . of course, it is all a lot of red tape. I have a cousin in the government, and he will surely be able to help."

"How do you know Rea won't get tired of Japan in a few years and go back to America?" Midori asked innocently. "She may have a boyfriend waiting there."

Lady Sachiko snorted a Japanese equivalent of "baloney.' "Rea-san will stay in Japan and in time become a proper Japanese," she stated. "Now, you must promise to stay with us here in Matsuyashiki for a few days. Midori and I will not let you go so easily."

Rea thought she detected a pleased gleam in Lady Sachiko's eyes, but wasn't sure. Thanking the old lady, she telephoned Janet Wynn with the news that she was to stay in Kyoto.

"Have you and Ivan patched things up?" Janet asked bluntly.

"Yes. I'll tell you everything later," Rea promised.

"You sound happy. Only . . ." Janet hesitated. "Be sure this is what you want, Rea."

Rea had never been more sure of anything in her life. The only cloud on her horizon was the news that Ivan had suddenly gone to Osaka on business. She could hardly wait for evening, and Ivan's return. Her cheeks flushed warmly as she thought of the night to come. No matter how long they lived, she would never be tired of waiting for him . . . or of welcoming him!

Finally, evening came. It did not bring Ivan, however Lady Sachiko told Rea that while she and Midori were changing for dinner Ivan had telephoned to say that he had some pressing business, and he might stay the night in Osaka.

Rea wondered if her disappointment showed. She was silent all through dinner, and when Hideo arrived, later that evening, she felt envious of the obvious joy in Midori's eyes. She gave herself a mental shake. She was acting like a love-starved teenager. Ivan had responsibilities. He'd be back soon, and when he was . . .

She went to bed around eleven, after Hideo's departure. However, tonight she couldn't sleep. The sleeping quilt seemed empty without the lean, muscular body stretched next to her. Finally, shortly after midnight, she got up and took a walk in the garden. But the balmy night air and the August stars that shone down on her hurt more than they helped. "I miss you," she whispered into the night. "I wish you were here, Ivan. I wish you would come home. . . ."

As if in answer to her wish, she heard the wheels of a car grating down the gravel pathway to Matsuyashiki. "Ivan!" she exclaimed. Wanting her as she wanted him, he had driven down from Osaka tonight instead of waiting for the morning.

Heedless of appearances, she ran through the garden in her bare feet, and had almost reached the courtyard when she heard Jiiya draw back the gate. Then she heard the servant's astonished cry: "Your Lordship the Baron!"

The baron! Rea stopped where she was, at the edge of the chrysanthemum garden. From there, she could see a cab in the driveway, and the driver getting out to open the back door. A slender, stoop-shouldered man got out. He seemed exhausted.

In spite of the hour, the servants had poured out to greet the master of Matsuyashiki. Lady Sachiko was there as well . . . and, behind her, Midori.

"Welcome home, brother," Lady Sachiko said, her gentle voice surprised. "You are home earlier than expected. Why didn't you telephone us and tell us you were coming? Ivan could have picked you up at Osaka Airport!"

"I didn't want anyone to know of my return. Ivan knows I am back . . . but he is needed in Osaka." His voice, Rea noted, was harsh. She hesitated, wondering whether to come forward and be introduced, or to slip back to her room. As she hesitated, the baron said, "Midori . . . the rest of you . . . I am sorry to have awakened you. Go back to bed. Sister," he added, "I need to speak with you. Come into the garden."

Rea realized that she couldn't go back to her room without disclosing where she was. The baron was too close to her, and now Lady Sachiko joined him. "Is something the matter?" Lady Sachiko was asking worriedly.

"We are ruined."

Though he spoke quietly, the baron's tone was riddled with despair. Rea heard Lady Sachiko suck in her breath.

"How? Why? It is impossible!"

"In business, everything rests on one thing . . . our good name," Baron Akira said. "Our honor has been soiled, sister."

In a low, harsh voice the baron told his story. The company had had a trusted employee, and he had been sent to the United States to negotiate a contract with the company that employed Jim Hume. This man had not negotiated in good faith. He had accepted bribes . . . payoffs.

"Now he has been exposed! He is being investigated by the American government . . . and so are we!"

Lady Sachiko's entire body seemed to sag. "Merciful Heaven," she moaned. "It will be a scandal!"

"I wanted you to know before the newspapers publish the story. They will, soon. That is why I came back so quickly . . . and why Ivan is in Osaka. We must make absolutely certain that there is no other taint on our honor. We must investigate our company records."

Rea closed her eyes, thinking of what the media would do to the Akiras. No saying was as true as the one about the top dog being hated by the rest of the pack. Sensing that the once-proud Akiras were down and out, the pack would close in for the kill. And Ivan . . .

"Only one thing can save us now," the baron was saying. "That is the intercession of our business associates. I hope that da Silva will stand by me, for one. If he vouches for me, we may still manage to salvage something."

"But . . . will he help?" Lady Sachiko asked.

"Why should he not help? His daughter will marry my son." Still talking, the two moved past Rea towards the house.

Rea stood stock-still. She was drained of all emotion except one—despair. Now Ivan couldn't ask his father to allow him to end his engagement to Catherina. Only the da Silvas could save the proud House of Akira. "Ivan . . ." she said mournfully.

Now she knew why he hadn't come back to Kyoto tonight. How could he face her with this news? What could he say? And what if he did see her and decided to give

Catherina up . . . even though this would be the ruin of his family?

"He couldn't do it. And even if he did . . . he'd end up hating himself, and me," she whispered to the still night air. "He'd hate me for destroying his honor and his family."

She could not let him be tempted to make a choice like that. She must leave Matsuyashiki before he returned. And it wasn't only for his sake that she must go. If he told her that he couldn't leave Catherina because of his family's honor, she wouldn't be able to let him go, she thought. She had to leave without seeing him. She had to . . .

For a moment, Rea had the impulse to pack her things and call a taxi, but that would be a terrible breach of etiquette. She would leave in the morning, pretending that nothing was wrong.

Rea sighed deeply, and there were tears in her eyes that blurred the splendor of the moon riding the clouds over the tall pines. "It was a wonderful dream," she whispered, "but that's all it could ever be. Now I have the rest of my life to live through, somehow, without him."

- 17 -

THE NEXT MORNING, Lady Sachiko looked hollow-eyed, and her face was puffy, as if she had cried all night. She still managed to muster a smile as she hugged Rea goodbye.

"I am sorry you are leaving us so soon, Rea-san," she said. "I will always remember what you did for Midori. Come again . . . soon!"

Rea knew she would never see Matsuyashiki again. She bit her lip to force back tears as she and Midori hugged goodbye. Then she realized that the baron had appeared on the scene. She bowed deeply as they were introduced.

"I have heard about you," he said, in English. "I have wanted to meet you very much." His eyes said plainly that in other circumstances, he would have liked to know her better.

Rea knew then that some intuition had made the baron aware of her feelings for Ivan. This strengthened her resolve to go . . . at once.

When she finally walked into the Wynns' apartment, later that morning, she found Janet hanging up the phone.

"What's going on?" Janet asked with a frown. "That was Ivan, calling from Kyoto. He wants you to telephone him right away. I thought everything was fine between you two."

Rea ignored the last comment. "The baron arrived home last night," she said.

"I know. It's all over the front pages." Janet held out a copy of the *Daily,* and Rea saw the black headlines which screamed: "Multibillion Business Loses Credibility." "You should see the rest of them. The *Japan Times,* the *Asahi.* It is a frightful scandal."

Rea forced herself to read the article carefully. Substantially, the report told her the same thing that Baron Akira had said last night. A trusted Akira Industries employee had tried to line his pockets in America. Exposed, he had confessed to taking bribes from firms not only in America but all over Europe. He had strongly implicated others in the firm.

Rea put the paper down. "They're going to crucify the Akiras," she moaned.

"That's big business. Once the top dog falls . . . the question is, what about you?" Janet moved over to the kitchen and momentarily emerged holding two cups of black coffee. "You're still in love with Ivan Akira, aren't you?"

It was useless to lie to Jan. "Yes . . . and he with me. But I'm bowing out." As Jan's eyes widened in dismay, Rea told her what she had overheard in the garden. "I can't help him in any way except by leaving him free to marry Catherina and salvage the good name of the firm," she said. "It's the only thing I can . . ."

Her words died away as the phone began to shrill. Agony lanced through Rea as her eyes met Janet's. Then Janet nodded and went to answer the phone. Rea heard her talking. "No . . . I'm sorry, Ivan. Not yet. Yes, I'll tell her." Then she heard the click of the receiver being returned to its cradle.

"Aren't you going to talk with him?" Rea heard Janet ask. "At least give him the choice of what to do or what not to do. I once told you that Ivan Akira was not right for you, but I think I was wrong. I have a feeling that the man genuinely loves you. If you walk out on him now, won't he think you're deserting him when he needs help the most?"

Rea covered her face with her hands, but when she dropped them, her eyes were dry. "I can't help that. It's the only way, I tell you. The Japanese aren't the only ones with honor, Janet. If I let Ivan walk away from his family now . . ." She got up. "Janet, you've been my friend so long, please, please do me one last favor. Telephone Ivan for me at Matsuyashiki. Tell him . . . tell him I've decided not to see him again."

Janet said nothing.

"If he interprets it the way I think he will, he'll be disgusted with me . . . and maybe the disgust will make him strong enough to help his family," Rea whispered. "I—I want to be alone now. Please." Turning her back on Janet, she slowly went to her room and sat down on her bed. Then she spied a long, slender envelope on top of her pile of manuscript.

It was the awaited letter from Inariyama. Rea opened it and read through it . . . the generous terms, the offer that had made her deliriously happy only a day ago. Yet, now she realized that even this was not for her.

"I can't take this offer now," she whispered brokenly. "If I do, I'll see him, and he'll see me. Even if he's married, he won't have a moment's peace, and eventually we'll find our way together again." Dimly, she realized that though other men might be unfaithful, Ivan could not divide his loyalties. Eventually, their love would drive a wedge between Ivan and his family . . . just as the love between Alexandra and the Bamboo Baron had caused so much trouble and pain.

Gently, Rea folded Inariyama's letter, and then tore it up into small, neat shreds, which she threw away. I am throwing away my life, she thought dully. My work and Ivan . . . I am leaving them both. Now she truly knew why Alexandra had gone, and how she must have felt. Suddenly, unable to bear it, she rested her face in her hands and wept.

Rea stayed in her room till Jan came knocking, telling her that she had spoken with Ivan. "He didn't argue with me—he seemed numb," she said. "Rea, are you sure . . . ?"

"I'm sure," Rea said though she knew that she was lying.

She telephoned Inariyama before her resolve could weaken, and felt fresh pain at the surprise and unhappiness expressed by the educator. "It was to be expected," he said with a sigh, "but somehow I had hoped . . . Well, you must do what's best for you. Are you returning to the States?"

Rea telephoned the airlines that day, to confirm her return flight. Within ten days, she would leave Japan, she thought as she hung up from that telephone call. I must finish up my business here . . . and my book. I must pack.

Her first draft was finished within the next few days. During this time, Rea was terrified that Ivan might telephone her . . . or worse, come to see her. He left her alone, however, and she knew that her leaving him must have hurt a great deal. Well, better to seem as though she was betraying him than to actually do him harm by her presence. Daily, news of the Akira scandal filled the papers. The entire company was being investigated, she read, and great business losses were resulting from this. "Akiras Ruined?" one headline shouted. Another held a more promising note: "Business Community Concede Not All Akiras' Fault . . ."

Everything she did reminded her of Ivan. Packing offered no respite. The photos she had taken were all somehow related to Ivan. There was the photo she had taken at the Kin-Bara that night . . . the snapshots of Osaka Castle. Would she ever forget what he had told her there about the lovers who had walked beneath the huge stones taken out of the Inland Sea? "A place to love and a place to die . . ." Oh, Ivan!

Rea realized that she had to break the tension somehow, or go insane. Suddenly, she knew what she must do. She had promised to visit Nando-*sensei* again. . . . She would go now, today.

Only a few hours later, Rea's tentative knocking at the old wooden gate brought a quick response from Mrs. Nando. Expressing pleasure at seeing Rea, the old lady bowed many times over the flowers she had brought.

"How very beautiful . . . how well the yellow of the chrysanthemums goes with the white of the lilies," the old lady said. Her eyes sparkled with genuine pleasure. "I will arrange them at once in my husband's studio. You will stay and speak with him? We have often thought of you, Rea-san."

Rea felt herself relax, become warm and tranquil, as she listened to the old lady's hearty welcome and followed her through the tiny garden into the house, to the artist's studio. After exchanging bows and compliments, Nando looked keenly at Rea.

"Is all well with you?" he asked.

She smiled. "Very well, *sensei*. I have finished my book, and leave in only a few days. I have come to say goodbye."

"I must have known you were coming, because I felt inspired to write a poem about chrysanthemums," Nando said with a pleased smile. Mrs. Nando now came in, carrying a vase and the flowers. She set the vase on the *to-konoma* and began to arrange the chrysanthemums and the lilies.

"I will always treasure your gift to me," Rea said. She smiled at the old man, but he did not smile back.

"You don't smile with your eyes any more, Rea-san." She turned, restless, and watched the old lady carefully positioning her flowers.

"I'm really fine. How about your work, *sensei?*"

"I work a little . . . sleep a little . . . meditate a little, which sometimes means the same as sleep." He chuckled. "At my age, sadness and joy are about the same thing, but when one is young . . ." He paused. "Are you glad to leave this country?"

"No." Rea dropped her voice. "No, I am not glad, *sensei*. But I have to."

"When one writes poetry or a book, one must go beyond the sense of happy or sad, beautiful or ugly. One must achieve 'muga,' or selflessness." His eyes were on her, gentle eyes which said that he understood. "Don't be afraid of sadness, Rea-san. It won't stay with you forever. Eventually, it and all your other memories will make you a stronger person."

Rea felt her heartache lift just a little. She could not yet quite understand what Nando had meant by "selflessness," but the tranquility of the little room, the warmth of the two old people and the beauty of brush and flowers before her soaked into her like needed rain after drought.

Impulsively, she said, "I'm glad I am here with you today, even if it is only to say goodbye."

"A short visit," Nando-*sensei* said gently, "but maybe that is enough. There is a haiku by Buson which says, 'A short night . . . the peony opened during that time.' In your short weeks with us, my friend, you have become a woman of insight and worthy of respect. We do not wish to see you go, my wife and I, and we will not forget you."

- 18 -

WHEN REA LEFT Nando's little house, she felt spiritually refreshed. The brief hour she had spent with the master and his wife had made her realize that no matter what the consequences, her stay in Japan, her meeting Ivan, had been right. She hoped that Nando-*sensei* was correct in saying that someday, sadness would leave her. Maybe one day, far in the future, she would be able to think of Ivan without the terrible ache of loneliness that seemed always to be with her.

Back at the Wynns' that evening, she found herself looking forward to going out with them for a farewell celebration. As they were getting ready, the doorbell rang.

Rea hurried to answer the door, then exclaimed, "Midori!"

"Excuse me for coming without warning, Rea-san." The small girl's face was frigidly formal. "There's something I need to ask you."

"I was going to telephone you and Lady Sachiko before I left . . ." She stopped awkwardly, seeing the hostility in Midori's eyes. Rea reminded herself she couldn't expect anything else. Midori must see her as a traitress.

"I see that you are well," Midori went on curtly. "I am sure you are glad to go back to the States."

"Er . . . won't you come in and have a drink?" Tucker asked nervously from behind Rea. Midori ignored him.

"I didn't expect that *you* would behave as you did! Everyone else, yes . . . especially that cold-blooded Catherina! But I always thought you loved my brother. I didn't expect you to stab him in the back."

Words of explanation tumbled to her lips, but Rea forced them back. It was just as well that Midori keep thinking the worst of her. "I did what I thought was best," she managed to reply quietly. "If that's all you came to say . . ."

Midori's lip quivered, and Rea turned quickly away. The tranquility she had found at Nando-san's house had been shattered by Midori's arrival. "You said something about asking me a question," she finally said.

Instead of replying to that, Midori began to speak in a low, halting voice. "The Akiras have never had their honor blackened like this before. Yes, we are ruined. This morning, there was the news that an investigation into our company records shows that there is other evidence of wrongdoing." Rea drew in her breath sharply. "Of all our former friends, only Hideo's family stands by us."

"But . . . surely, the da Silvas are still your friends?"

"Diego da Silva supported my family until now, because if the Akiras went down, he would lose all the investments he has made in our company. But now he will wash his hands of us, as Catherina has done."

In spite of the whirling in her brain, Rea's mind fastened on that one bit of news. "Catherina has broken with Ivan?"

"What else? She never loved my brother, and only wanted to marry him because of our family standing." She glared at Rea. "That was what you wanted from Ivan, wasn't it? That's why you deserted him when he needed you so much."

"Midori, please!"

"It was all right for you to care for Ivan when he was the big baron's son, wasn't it? Now that he has nothing, you couldn't care less about him. What does it matter to you that he's ready to—" She stopped, a stricken look in her eyes. "I've said too much," she muttered.

"What do you mean? Desperate enough to do *what?*" Rea cried. Midori didn't answer, and Rea grabbed her hands. "What is Ivan planning to do?"

Dully, Midori said, "What do you think? He is Japanese. We have been disgraced by a stain on our honor. The only thing that will take away the stain is death."

"You can't mean he's going to kill himself!" Tucker gasped, and Rea felt her blood turn to ice. She felt her legs go rubbery under her, and she told herself firmly that she couldn't faint. Not now!

"Where is he?" she demanded.

"How do I know?" Midori was close to tears. "He left Matsuyashiki this morning, after telling Aunt Sachi good-bye. . . . I suspected something then! And some time later, I found his death poem in the Chrysanthemum Room. The room where *you* used to stay," she added to Rea.

His death poem! Warriors and aristocrats wrote a death poem before they died, in old Japan. Rea gritted her teeth against a wave of nausea. "We must find him! Don't you have any idea where he has gone?"

"I was hoping you might know. That's why I came here!" Midori fumbled in her pocketbook and produced a scrap of paper. "Satoh-san and some of the others are looking, and Aunt Sachi, and all the servants." She handed Rea the paper silently.

His death poem, Rea thought dully. Her eyes scanned the delicate Japanese characters. Although she was no great scholar of written Japanese, she could read this much. "Better to stop breathing that finds no place where it is good to love," the words told her. "Better to find a place where it is good to die."

"Could he have gone outside of Osaka?" Tucker was asking Midori worriedly. "Think! I'll drive you anywhere you want to go."

A place to love and a place to die. Think, Rea told herself desperately. Where had she heard those words before?

"Perhaps the Chrysanthemum inn . . . or Nando-*sensei*'s place. That is in Ashiya," Midori was saying.

Memory came to Rea with sudden clarity. She remembered warm grass, flowers, the ripple of water, and pain in her ankle. "Osaka Castle," she whispered.

Midori and Tucker looked puzzled. "I'll . . . go on to Osaka Castle. You go to the Chrysanthemum inn with Tucker," Rea told her.

Midori nodded. "I pray one of us finds him before it is too late," she whispered.

As soon as Rea paid the cab driver who'd taken her to Osaka Castle, she started across the park at a run. Her shoes slipped on the dew-wet grass, so she took them off and ran in her bare feet. She raced past the closed, barred souvenir stands and across the moat, then slid her shoes back on so that she could climb the winding gravel path.

The *kendo* school had closed its doors long since, and the pathway was deserted. She gasped for breath as she raced up the flights of stone stairs, and again through the winding pathway that led to the enclosure surrounding the castle.

Inside the enclosure, restaurants were still doing business. Customers, enjoying tea and noodles, looked at her, surprised, as she burst asking whether or not they had seen a tall man with green eyes.

"Can't be sure, ma'am . . . lots of people come to see the castle," one of the diners finally volunteered. He added that the castle had been closed for at least an hour.

It couldn't be closed! But when Rea finally reached the massive wooden gate of the castle, it was shut and barred. In a frenzy of despair, she pounded her fists on the ungiving wood.

"Open . . . please open!" she called.

Sobbing, she slammed the palms of her hands against the door. "Oh, please . . ."

Someone called to her from one of the food shops. "The guards close the castle down at sunset, and it'll stay shut till the morning. What's wrong? Did you lose something inside the castle?"

Rea slumped against the gate. Either Ivan wasn't in there, or . . . he wasn't alive. She pushed icy hands against her hot cheeks, tried to think. The castle was closed, but . . . She now remembered the huge boulders, part of the original Osaka Castle, which stood outside the enclosure.

Perhaps . . . ! She ran through the enclosure and out into the darkness beyond. The old stones stood in shadow, and she could not see very well as she hurried up to them. Then her heart jumped into her throat. A tall man was leaning against the stones.

"Ivan?" she whispered.

His voice was rough, unwelcoming. "What are you doing here, Rea?"

She didn't care whether he wanted to see her or not. He

was here; he was alive! She ran to him and reached out to clasp him around the waist, but he took her hands in his and held her off. She clung shamelessly to his hands, laughing aloud in a dizzy, breathless gratitude.

"You're all right!"

"Of course I'm all right." His voice was irritated. His tone was the old one, full of mockery. "Why wouldn't I be all right?"

She was suddenly confused, and pulled her hands away from him. "I . . . I thought . . ."

"I'm sure you considered many things," he said. "Now that things are better, you have come running back to me. Well, I don't want you, Rea."

He turned, dismissing her. She felt confused and uncertain, worrying that now that she had found him, he might discover another place in which to kill himself. "Where are you going?" she asked.

"To a bar . . . or a nightclub. There, the women don't tell lies," he said curtly. "When a nightclub hostess entertains a man, she is honest about what she is doing."

Her face flushed in the darkness. Well, he had the right to think that of her. If only she was sure he would be all right. "Will you let me go with you?"

He looked at her in surprise, and suddenly laughed, a harsh, brutal bark. "You don't understand things very well, do you? Well, let me spell it out for you." He reached out suddenly, pulling her to him so roughly that she gasped in pain. "Does that hurt? I hope so. I hope it hurts you to the bottom of your cheating, conniving little heart! I thought—I really believed!—you loved me. I was ready to give everything to you and for you. And then, at the first sign of trouble, you ran!"

There was raw pain in his voice, and she could not stand it. "I came back, Ivan. I learned—"

"I know what you learned! You found out that just today, the company was cleared of wrongdoing . . . that it was only that one employee who was indicted! I don't know how you got hold of that piece of news, Rea. We only learned it this morning ourselves, and the papers haven't yet been told. But I'm sure that nothing aids the quest for truth like a woman's greed. Here you are, wanting your meal ticket again."

She listened to his words in horror. The company honor was intact, then! But Midori had said . . . and yet, Midori undoubtedly knew that the company had been cleared! She shook her head, trying to make sense of jumbled bits and pieces of what Midori had told her, and then she remembered what Midori had said about Catherina.

"Catherina and you . . ." she began.

Even in the darkness, she could see his lip curl. "Catherina and you are two of a kind, my dear. She, too, deserted when the storm came. By now, she's probably decided on some other fine 'catch.' She, at least, had the intelligence not to come whining back to me."

Suddenly, Rea felt exhausted and drained. There was no use trying to convince Ivan of what she had meant to do. No use explaining why she had come racing to Osaka Castle. Why should he believe anything she said? To him, doubtless, she looked like the most conniving, mercenary woman on earth.

She drew a shuddery breath. "I am glad about your firm, Ivan. You probably won't believe it, but until now, I didn't know that everything was . . . was well."

He let go of her, and seemed to struggle to control himself. "If you must know, everything isn't that well. We have had heavy losses because of our employee's dishonesty. My father and I have planned new approaches to the business." He paused, then said abruptly, "I hear you are returning to your country." She nodded, unable to speak. "You decided not to accept Inariyama's offer, then. Or was that a lie . . . like everything else?"

In the grass someplace near them, a cricket began to chirp. The sound made Rea feel suddenly old. Autumn was coming. For her, summer seemed far away, a warm, happy time which would never come again. She remembered the haiku on Ivan's wall about the short day of summer.

"So this is goodbye," Ivan said harshly. "Perhaps you will have the courtesy to telephone Aunt Sachi and Midori. They still think the world of you. They know nothing, though I think Midori guesses. She came on me one day while I was writing some rather stupid poetry . . ."

Suddenly, illumination flashed through Rea's mind. "The death poem!" she murmured. "The poem Midori showed me!"

"*Death* poem? Have you gone quite mad?" Ivan demanded. "And when would Midori have showed you anything? She is in Osaka, shopping. I told her I was coming to Osaka Castle while she—"

"She said you were going to kill yourself. She sent me here. Oh, how could she!" Rea moaned.

"You aren't making sense, Rea. Explain yourself," Ivan said.

Rea explained what Midori had told her. Ivan's tone was incredulous when he asked, "Why on earth would she have lied like that?"

"Because she knows I love you," Rea said. "I am sorry about the dramatics tonight, Ivan." She laughed suddenly, a sad little laugh. "She probably felt that she was doing us a favor . . . the way I did Hideo and her a favor."

"You still are not making sense."

She drew a deep breath. "Ivan, I heard your father and your aunt talking. I didn't mean to, but I did. I heard the baron say that the only way the family honor could be saved was for da Silva to stand by you . . . and that because you were to marry Catherina, he would probably do so. I . . . I decided that I had to leave at once, making you believe I no longer loved you. I didn't want you to have to choose between me and your family."

"You expect me to believe that?" Ivan asked.

The air around them was suddenly hushed. Even the cricket had fallen silent. "I don't know. I can't help what you believe." She realized she had wrapped her arms around herself in the old gesture of uncertainty.

"Don't do that!" he said sharply. "Rea . . ."

Suddenly, she could not stand it. She could not remain there and have him look at her with contempt and hatred. She turned from him blindly and began to hurry away. Gravel crunched under her feet, but she could not hear the sound, could barely feel the ground. Like some doomed creature, she made her way through the darkness, half-blinded by the tears that were streaming down her face. She wept soundlessly, feeling as if an ocean of tears were locked someplace inside her.

Well, she had years in which to cry them all!

She didn't see the first of the stone steps before her, and stumbled. For a frightening second, she felt as if she were falling forward into space, and then he was holding her. "Be careful," he said. "You don't want to spoil your act by falling."

She looked into his face and saw the change there. "You said that to me . . . the first time you kissed me," she whispered. He kissed her again, his lips achingly sweet on hers. She knew he believed her then, and began to cry harder as she clung to him. She couldn't get enough of the feel of him or of his arms around her.

"I have missed you so much," he said against her lips. "I couldn't believe it when you walked out of my life, but . . . well, I thought it over, and there was Catherina leaving me, as well. I told myself that I couldn't blame you, but I did. God, how much I blamed you!"

You should have known," Rea said. He brushed the tears away with his fingertips and his lips. "You know I wouldn't have cared if you didn't have a cent in the world."

"I know now. And you turned down Inariyama's offer because of me, didn't you? You must call him tonight. He will be delighted to have you back with him. After all, his school might be the next building I design."

"Design, Ivan?" A happiness was sweeping through her, filling her with heady warmth.

He smiled at her, eager as a boy. "That's one of the new ideas Father and I had! We agree that putting all our capital into industry is foolish. We are going to build apartments on some of our family land . . . not just any apartments, but structures of grace and beauty. I will be in charge of designing and building them. It will be work for my soul."

Too glad for words, she snuggled close against him. To her surprise, he put her sternly from him. "It's work I can't do alone, however. You will, naturally, marry me." He sounded like the arrogant Akira of days past, and Rea raised her eyebrows at him. He tried to curl his mouth into one of his mocking smiles but failed utterly, the more so when she pulled his head down to her and kissed the corner of his lips.

"I love you," she sighed in utmost content.

"And I adore you."

Their shadows blended again, and Rea felt that the new moon looked benignly down on them, this newest pair of lovers to make their vows near the ancient, noble castle. Rea sighed again, deeply, and knew that she had found security, peace and love—at last—in this flower-scented land.

QUESTIONNAIRE

1. How many romances do you *read* each month? ______

2. How many of these do you *buy* each month? ______

3. Do you read primarily
   - ☐ novels in romance lines like SECOND CHANCE AT LOVE
   - ☐ historical romances
   - ☐ bestselling contemporary romances
   - ☐ other ______

4. Were the love scenes in this novel (this is book # ______)
   - ☐ too explicit
   - ☐ not explicit enough
   - ☐ tastefully handled

5. On what basis do you make your decision to buy a romance?
   - ☐ friend's recommendation
   - ☐ bookseller's recommendation
   - ☐ art on the front cover
   - ☐ description of the plot on the back cover
   - ☐ author
   - ☐ other ______

6. Where did you buy this book?
   - ☐ chain store (drug, department, etc.)
   - ☐ bookstore
   - ☐ supermarket
   - ☐ other ______

7. Mind telling your age?
   - ☐ under 18
   - ☐ 18 to 30
   - ☐ 31 to 45
   - ☐ over 45

8. How many SECOND CHANCE AT LOVE novels have you read?
   - ☐ this is the first
   - ☐ some (give number, please ______)

9. How do you rate SECOND CHANCE AT LOVE vs. competing lines?
   - ☐ poor
   - ☐ fair
   - ☐ good
   - ☐ excellent

10. Check here if you would like to
    - ☐ receive the SECOND CHANCE AT LOVE Newsletter

Fill-in your name and address below:

name: ______

street address: ______

city ______ state ______ zip ______

Please share your other ideas about romances with us on an additional sheet and attach it securely to this questionnaire.

PLEASE RETURN THIS QUESTIONNAIRE TO:
SECOND CHANCE AT LOVE, THE BERKLEY/JOVE PUBLISHING GROUP
200 Madison Avenue, New York, New York 10016